# MIKE LUPICA

# ANGERS

## PLAY MAKERS

SCHOLASTIC INC.

No part of this publication may be reproduced, stored in a retrieval system, or transmitted in any form or by any means, electronic, mechanical, photocopying, recording, or otherwise, without written permission of the publisher. For information regarding permission, write to Scholastic Inc., Attention: Permissions Department, 557 Broadway, New York, NY 10012.

This book was originally published in hardcover by Scholastic Press in 2013.

ISBN 978-0-545-38180-2

Copyright © 2013 by Mike Lupica. All rights reserved. Published by Scholastic Inc. SCHOLASTIC and associated logos are trademarks and/or registered trademarks of Scholastic Inc.

12 11 10 9 8 7 6 5 4 3 2 1    14 15 16 17 18 19/0

Printed in the U.S.A.  40
This edition first printing, February 2014

Book design by Phil Falco

*To Christopher, Alex, Zach, Hannah Grace, and the former Taylor McKelvy, of course. All of you are my own constant proof that God smiles.*

## BOOKS BY
# MIKE LUPICA

# 1

Just like that, it was basketball season.

It was basketball season this fast, so soon after football. Almost *too* soon for Ben McBain, even though he usually couldn't wait for the next season in sports to begin.

When you were eleven like he was, that was the beauty of sports, you didn't have to wait until next year, not if you played football and basketball and baseball the way he did in Rockwell.

Sometimes you barely had to wait at all, even if people in Rockwell still hadn't stopped talking about the way football had ended for Ben and the rest of the Rockwell Rams in the championship game against Parkerville.

So two weeks from when Ben had hit Sam Brown for a touchdown on the last play of the championship game, Ben and Sam and Cooper (Coop) Manley were on their way to Darby, next town over, for their only preseason scrimmage, one week before the season started for real, Rockwell vs. Darby again, this time in the gym at Rockwell Middle School.

They were all piled into the backseat of Mrs. Manley's car for the short ride, knowing that it was only supposed to be a scrimmage, but also knowing Darby *was* their biggest rival in just about everything.

Knowing they'd want to beat Darby even if it was just a pie-eating contest.

"Are we ready for this?" Coop said now. "Because I don't know if I'm ready for this."

He had one window, Sam had the other, Ben was in between them. You could be the biggest star on the field, the way Ben had been against Parkerville, but when you were small, the way Ben was small, you still got stuck with the middle seat.

"Gotta admit," Ben said, "this is one time when even I would have been fine with a little more of a break. That way we could have celebrated for a few more days. Like guys do after they win the Stanley Cup and they travel all around with it."

"Same," Sam said. "Even though Coop would still be posing on the field next to our trophy if we didn't practically drag him away."

"He did look awfully darn cute," Mrs. Manley said from the front.

"Mom, stop," Coop said.

They were passing through Darby's downtown area, which was even smaller than Rockwell's.

"Hey," Coop said, "I hear you guys on this. It was only the greatest football game in the history of our town, even if it was a bunch of sixth graders. I'm totally not done talking about it yet."

"Now *there's* a shocker," Ben said. "You not wanting to stop talking, I mean."

"About anything," Sam said.

"Some people just have more to say than others," Coop said. "Isn't that what you've always told me, Mom?"

Ben looked up at the rearview mirror, could see Mrs. Manley smiling. "Honestly, dear?" she said. "Sometimes I just say that hoping you'll stop talking."

"Mrs. Manley!" Sam said. "From downtown."

"Have your fun," Coop said. "This will all be in my book someday."

"Whoa," Ben said. "You plan to write one before you, like, *read* one?"

They all laughed. Happy, as always, to be in one another's company. Happy to have the usual chirp going on between them. Happy that they had a game to play, even if it did seem as if they were coming straight to the scrimmage against Darby from that amazing football game against Parkerville.

Sometimes Ben wished his whole world could be Saturdays exactly like this.

The backseat got quiet for a moment, even Coop. It was Sam who spoke next.

"Before we do start hoops today," he said, "anybody besides me wondering how we *can* possibly top what we just did in football?"

Ben said, "We'll just do what we always do."

Coop said, "I know I know what we always do . . . but help me out here."

"We'll show up and hope something great happens," Ben said.

"And then *make* something great happen," Sam said.

It had happened during the football season, at least the season that really began about halfway through when Coach O'Brien put Ben in at quarterback and he showed Coach and everybody else that he wasn't too small to be a quarter-back after all. The Rams were losing by three touchdowns to Parkerville in the regular-season game the two teams had played, but somehow Ben — with a lot of help from Sam, the best receiver on the team and in the league — brought them all the way back.

The Rams never lost another game after that.

Finally it was the championship game, the rematch with Parkerville, and they were down four points and down to their last play. Only it turned out to be their version of the most famous pass in college football history, at least as far as Ben was concerned: The Doug Flutie pass Ben had always imag-ined himself making.

His dad had played with Flutie at Boston College, when Flutie became the quarterback who was supposed to be too small before he proved the whole world wrong. His dad was a defensive back on that BC team, so he was there the day in Miami, after Thanksgiving, when Flutie made his desperate, last-play-of-the-game throw to beat the University of Miami, throwing it half the length of the field to his best friend, Gerard Phelan, when nobody thought BC still had a chance.

The way nobody thought little Doug Flutie could ever win a Heisman Trophy.

There had been other Hail Mary passes in football history, never one more famous than that. But Ben made his, to his best friend, against Parkerville, running around in the backfield to buy himself time, to give Sam time to get behind the defense, then throwing it as far as he could and watching Sam catch it like a center fielder catching a fly ball, pressing the ball to the front of his jersey and then falling back into the end zone with the play that gave the Rockwell Rams the championship.

Even the town paper covered the game, calling Ben "Ben McMiracle" in the headlines.

Ben leaned back, closed his eyes now, remembered all of it: The crazy celebration on the field that began with his mad dash to get to Sam. All the posing they did with the championship trophy. The party back at Ben's house that ended up spilling across the street to the field across from the house that all of Ben's friends called "McBain Field," Ben and Sam and Coop and Shawn O'Brien out there until dark still throwing a football around, not wanting the season to be over.

Before Ben had finally gone to bed that night, Sam Brown had called him on the telephone, and said, "It really happened, right?"

Ben had said, "It happened."

"So it wasn't a dream?" Sam had said, and Ben had laughed and said, "Well, it kind of was."

Only then, before they'd even had a chance to catch their breath, it really was basketball season. Tryouts for the town team the next week, the team announced at the end of that week, then a week of practice. And that was why, two weeks after Ben threw it and Sam caught it against Parkerville, they were in Darby, a couple of blocks away from the gym at Darby Middle School.

Shawn O'Brien was meeting them there, his parents having driven him to the game. At first he wasn't going to go out for basketball, saying he'd never even tried out before. But Ben had seen enough in pickup games at school to know that he'd make a perfect power forward for them, or even a center when Coop sat down. So he talked Shawn into it, and then Shawn had crushed the tryouts, and not only had this year's Rockwell team gotten bigger because of Shawn, Ben knew it had gotten better.

Not only had he and Sam and Coop gained a friend because of the way everything had worked out in football, they'd gained a rebounder and low-post shooter.

Coop poked Ben and said, "You sleeping?"

"Wide awake," Ben said.

"Good," Coop said. "'Cause when we get out of the car, it *is* basketball season, dude. And we *are* playing Darby. Which means that even though it's just supposed to be a dopey scrimmage, we need to send a message."

Somehow Ben knew to look to his right, where he saw Sam grinning at him.

"And what would that be, exactly?" Sam said. "This message we need to send?"

"Mrs. Manley?" Ben said, "Could you turn down the radio so we can all hear the message we need to send to Darby today?"

Ben and Sam stared at Coop now as he stared out the window, frowning like he was trying to solve a math problem in his head.

"We're all waiting," Sam said.

"I'm thinking," Coop said.

"Oh, happy day!" Mrs. Manley said. "My boy, he's thinking! It's . . . it's like an early Christmas . . . *miracle*!"

"You're not funny, Mom."

"I know, dear. You get that from me."

"Now *that's* funny," Sam said.

"You two back here, shut up and listen," Coop said. "Here's the message we need to send: that we're gonna be the big dogs in our league again this year, same as we were in football."

"That's it, dog?" Sam said. "*That's* the message?"

Ben made a growling noise, the kind you'd hear from a small dog.

"Make your little jokes," Coop said. "You know you're both thinking the exact same thing."

"All due respect, Coop?" Ben said. "No one thinks the way you do."

Coop acted as if he hadn't heard. "It doesn't have to be an actual message," he said. "When they say on TV that one team is sending a message to the other, it's not like they spell it out the way you would in a text message."

"That's a good thing," Sam said. "Because with your texting skills, the message would be even harder to understand."

"Like with LOL," Ben said, grinning.

"Oh," Coop said, "like I'm the only person on the planet who thought that meant 'lots of love.' Something I never get from you two, by the way."

Ben looked at Sam, confused. "Where do you suppose he gets an idea like that?"

*"From you two!"* Coop said.

They all laughed again, starting to get ready now, knowing they had a game to play. Mrs. Manley turned into the parking lot at Darby Middle School. They all could see the double doors to a gym where they'd played plenty of times before.

In the backseat, Ben put his hand out, something else he'd done plenty of times before. Then Sam's hand was on top of his, and Coop's was on top of Sam's, and it officially wasn't football season anymore.

They got out of the car and walked across the lot and into the gym and that was when Ben first saw Darby's new point guard, Chase Braggs.

And just like that, his season changed before it had even officially begun. The story of the day, of what was supposed to be just a scrimmage, wasn't Rockwell going up against its oldest rival.

It was Ben McBain finding out he had a new one.

# 2

It was Lily Wyatt who first told them about the basketball star their age who'd moved to Darby from someplace in Indiana.

But then Lily seemed to know about everything first, whether it was a new movie they all had to see or a new singer they all had to hear, or a hot new TV show or app or gadget or game.

She was an original member of what they all called the Core Four. Coop was the one who'd first started calling them that. He was a Yankee fan, and he knew all about how Derek Jeter and Mariano Rivera and Jorge Posada and Andy Pettitte had won a bunch of World Series together and been called the Core Four of those teams. So now Lily, Ben, Sam, Coop were the Core Four, even if they only called themselves that in front of each other.

And Lily Wyatt, they all knew, was a lot more than just one of the guys, the coolest girl in their grade, and in Rockwell and — Ben was pretty sure — probably the coolest eleven-year-old girl on the planet.

She was also Ben's closest friend, even if he would never admit that to Sam or Coop. A girl friend. When he'd describe her that way, he'd always make sure to come to a complete stop between "girl" and "friend." Like he'd used a Pause button. Of course Sam never said it the same way, just to torture Ben. Always called her Ben's "girlfriend." One word. Knowing that Ben liked to have Lily called his girlfriend — one *terrible* word — about as much as he liked homework.

His friendship with Lily was just different. Different from what he had with Sam and Coop and Shawn, who really had changed the Core Four into five by the end of football. It was different even though they all went to school together and hung together and felt as if they were members of the world's most exclusive club for eleven-year-olds.

The way Lily was different, pretty much from anybody Ben had ever known. She was also the person who knew Ben the best, even better than his mom and dad sometimes.

The way she found out about Chase Braggs was this:

She had a good friend in Darby she'd played against in travel soccer. The friend — her name was Molly Arcelus — had a brother on the sixth-grade basketball team, named Jeb, who came home from the first night of Darby's tryout talking about this new guy who'd blown them all away.

Since their dad was a stockbroker, Jeb had told his sister: "Dad ought to buy stock in this guy Chase."

Lily had called Ben right away, because she always called him right away when she had what she called "intel."

"There's always a new guy we're supposed to be worrying about in sports," Ben had said that night. "Or an old guy who grew over the summer. Or somebody who just flat-out got better. Whatever."

"No, this could be great, if this guy's as good as Molly's brother says he is," Lily had said. "You and this Chase could be like the Rockwell–Darby version of Kobe and LeBron."

She knew as much about sports as any guy he knew.

"First of all," Ben had said. "Kobe and LeBron isn't that big a rivalry, they never even played in the Finals against each other. But I know *you* know that, because you know everything."

"Okay, Bird and Magic, then!" Lily had said. "Who I actually didn't know all that much about till you made me watch that cool HBO movie about them."

"Man," Ben had said, "it sounds like this Chase guy is the best player you've never seen. What's his last name, again?"

"Braggs. Chase Braggs. Sounds kind of like a verb, right? Get it? Chase *Braggs*."

"You're doing a good enough job bragging on him yourself," Ben had said. "Somebody who's never even played a game yet around here."

"Listen, you know Jeb is good," Lily had said. "And he says Chase is off the hook."

"Who are you — Coop?" Ben had said, both of them knowing "off the hook" was one of Coop's favorite expressions.

"Be nice," Lily had said, "I'm just giving you a heads-up so you'll bring your A game to the scrimmage next week."

"No, Lils," Ben had said, "even though it's Darby I was just going to go with B-minus. Maybe a C-plus."

"Did I mention to the best point guard in the league that Chase was a point guard, too?" Lily had said.

"I think right after I said hello. And there's a lot of good point guards in the league besides me."

"Blah blah blah, Big Ben," she said. "Last year nobody in the league could get in front of you." Adding: "Like me in soccer."

He had known she was smiling at the other end of the phone even though he couldn't actually *see* her smiling. It was what she called him. Big Ben. Even though he was small for his age. Smaller than her.

A big thing with him.

"Lils," he had said, "do you really think I need somebody from the other team to fire me up?"

"Not trying to fire you up, dude. Just giving you a *heads-up*." Ben had pictured her still smiling as she said, "You're welcome."

"Seriously?" Ben had said. "How good can he be?"

He found out at Darby Middle School before the first quarter was over.

The Rams had the same coach for sixth-grade ball they'd had last season, Keith Wright having moved up to the next level right along with them.

It was a huge break, as far as all the guys on the team were concerned, most of them having played for Coach Wright in fifth grade.

They'd all decided last season they'd be perfectly happy playing for Coach Wright until they got to high school. He was still in his twenties, had played college ball at UConn — never a starter, he told them, but always in Coach Jim Calhoun's rotation, always getting his minutes — and wanted to be a college coach himself someday.

"Everybody's got their dreams," he'd told them last year. "Coaching in March Madness one day is mine."

He'd been a point guard at UConn, even though he was only 5-8, and still looked young enough to be playing college ball. Maybe even playing for Rockwell High School. His face always made Ben think of Will Smith. Coach was just shorter.

The thing Ben and his teammates liked the best about him? He loved basketball the way they did, seemed to smile the whole time he was on the court with them, even when he was telling them they'd messed up. And talked to them constantly about them playing it the right way.

Of course in the e-mails he sent out to the players and their parents, he said he wanted them to play the "Wright way."

Except that three minutes into the first scrimmage of the new season it was 12–2, Darby, and he'd been forced to call his first time-out of the season because Rockwell's Rams were playing the opposite of the right way. Going the wrong way. Fast.

"Okay," he said when they were all around him. "This is a good thing."

Coop, who played center, said, "You mean because we're not down 20–2 the way that guy is playing?"

That guy.

Chase Braggs.

"No," Coach said, "because now we've identified who we need to stop."

Ben had been guarding Chase. Or trying to. "I'll settle for slowing him down," he said. "Like a speed bump."

It had only been three minutes, and Ben wasn't about to lose his mind after three minutes of a scrimmage, but so far his main problem with Chase Braggs was this:

Everything Ben did on a basketball court, Chase seemed to be doing just a little better.

He wasn't that much bigger, but somehow used the size difference between them to his advantage every chance he'd gotten so far. He wasn't really all that much faster with the ball than Ben was, he just seemed faster right now, as if he were playing at a different speed than Ben and everybody else, and that meant Chase's own teammates, too.

He had eight of Darby's points, making two shots from the outside, driving past Ben for two layups, assisting on the other two Darby baskets. One was a pass from halfcourt to their center, who'd broken ahead of the pack. The other was a no-look bounce pass in traffic to Ryan Hurley, a kid they all knew from having played football against him.

"It's not just you, dude," Sam said in the huddle. "Ryan made me look like somebody'd Krazy-Glued my sneaks to the floor."

"Okay," Coach said, smiling. "Enough of this fascinating play-by-play. I want you all to relax and stop obsessing about the new guy. Everybody help Ben on defense whenever we can, because that's what we play, boys, against everybody. Help defense. And just keep trying to make the extra pass on offense. Don't worry about his stuff. Worry about ours."

Before they broke the huddle, Coach grabbed Ben and said, "You want, we can start messing around with our zone, I was gonna eventually do that, anyway."

"No," Ben said, "I got this."

And went back out there to match up with Chase Braggs. There were some things Ben would never say out loud, but knew in his heart. Like the way he really felt about Lily, who was right when she said Ben had been the best point guard in the league last season. Sam said it all the time, so did Coop, not just Lily. Ben never said it. But knew it was true. He'd been the best ball handler, the best passer of the ball. Maybe not the best shooter, but if you backed off him and dared him to put it up, he could make you pay, especially in a big spot.

Only today, in the only game that ever mattered to Ben McBain — the one he was playing — Chase Braggs was the best point guard in the gym, by a lot, the whole game running through him.

And worse?

He was playing to the crowd every chance he got.

Chase *Braggs*.

Yeah, it was like he was bragging on himself for real. Chase Braggs was good and knew it and wanted to make sure that people watching *knew* he knew it. Every time he made a pass or a shot he'd bob his head up and down and smile, like he was the boy with the right answer to every question in class.

15

Sometimes he'd look over into the crowd and point at a man and woman Ben assumed were his parents, the man pointing back at him. Or he'd run past his coach and slap him a quick low five. He didn't need to draw any more attention to himself, not the way he was schooling Ben and the rest of the Rams.

But he was. Not in a big, showy, obnoxious way. But it was like Chase wanted to control the ball and the spotlight at the same time.

Wanted all eyes on him at all times, like he thought he might end up on SportsCenter tonight, like he was starring in his own highlight reel.

After Chase had made his very first outside shot of the day, Ben slow getting around a screen, he heard Chase say this to one of his teammates:

"That's why they call me Chase. 'Cause guys have to chase me all day." Smiling and nodding as he did.

It was 26–6, Darby, by the end of the quarter, at which point Coach Wright put in their second unit, even though he never called it that. By then Ben was still scoreless, had just one assist, to Sam for a layup on a backdoor play of their own.

Ben had also turned the ball over three times, the last right before the quarter ended, taking his eyes off Chase just long enough at the top of the key, waiting for Coop to come up and set a screen. As he did, Chase's right hand flicked out, knocked the ball off Ben's dribble, pushing the ball ahead as he did. Ben had no chance to catch him, had to watch from halfcourt as Chase slowed up just enough that he got off his shot before the clock went to zeroes for the quarter, holding his shooting pose again, just long enough to make you notice he'd done it.

He wasn't pounding his chest the way guys in college or the pros did after a dunk. But the guy clearly liked to style. Had some stuff he was into.

Walking off the court, Sam said to Ben, "Like my dad says, not enough mustard in the world for that hot dog."

"And relish," Coop said. "And sauerkraut."

"Feeling pretty sour myself about now," Ben said.

Sam said, "It'll be different in the second half."

Ben said, "You sure of that?"

As it turned out the second half was pretty much a copy of the first, Chase Braggs doing what he wanted to do against Ben, getting his shots, making a behind-the-back pass to Ryan Hurley before his coach took him out for good early in the fourth quarter, since Darby was ahead by twenty points at the time.

Darby ended up winning, 55–38. Worst beatdown Ben could ever remember getting in basketball, from the time he and Sam and Coop had started playing fourth-grade ball at the Rockwell YMCA, which Ben's dad ran.

When it was over, Ben walked to the scorer's table, looked at the scorebook that Coach Wright's girlfriend kept at games, saw that Chase Braggs had scored twenty-four points even though he'd played just over half the game. Brenda, Coach's girlfriend and a former player herself, didn't keep assists for the other team, but Ben knew Chase had to have had at least ten. Maybe more.

Ben? He ended up with six points, two assists, knew that he'd turned the ball over half a dozen times. It was a lot. There had been games last season when he didn't turn it over at all.

There was no handshake line after the game for the two teams, not after a scrimmage. Even though the scrimmage suddenly felt like a lot more to Ben. Sam and Coop went over to talk to Ryan Hurley.

Ben was still standing in front of the scorer's table, just wanting to get to his dad's car, when he saw Chase Braggs walking toward him.

Chase still smiling.

Ben thinking: If I'd played the way he did today, I'd be smiling, too. But already thinking about knocking that smile off the guy's face the first chance he got.

Ben McBain hated to lose. In anything. Hated to lose as much as he loved to compete. But he knew there was a way to behave in sports, win or lose. Told himself to put on his fake smile and get it over with and get out of there.

Chase put out his right hand, which seemed to be about twice the size of Ben's, introduced himself. Ben did the same.

"Heard a lot about you," Chase Braggs said. "You really throw that pass in the championship game?"

"Lucky heave," Ben said. "Plus, the guy who caught it is the best receiver I'm ever gonna have."

"Not the way Ryan tells it," Chase said. "He said the only

guy who could have made that throw was the guy who made it."

"Sort of like the guy making all those shots against me today," Ben said.

They both shrugged, almost at the same moment, as if they'd run out of small talk. Or ways to blow smoke at each other.

"Well, I hope I can do that when you're playing your hardest," Chase Braggs said, and then said he'd see Ben when they played the next Saturday in Rockwell.

There was a ball just sitting there on the floor, just outside the three-point line. As Chase walked across to where his coach was waiting for him, he casually scooped up the ball, turned and squared up and fired one last shot that hit nothing but net, like it was as easy as making a layup.

Then he wagged his finger one more time the way he had in the game, kept walking.

Not even chasing after the ball, as if he knew somebody else would go pick it up later. Just turning and giving Ben one last wave, not to say good-bye, Ben knew, just to make sure that Ben had been watching.

Ben stood there and watched as Chase, hair almost as red as the red uniform he was wearing, got one last high five for the day, this one from his coach.

Ben feeling as if Chase had made one last shot on him, and thinking:

I *was* playing my hardest.

Sam and Coop rode home in Mrs. Manley's car, Shawn hitching a ride with them because his parents had to go watch one of Shawn's sisters play a soccer game. So Ben rode home with his dad, who'd shown up about five minutes before the opening tip.

It meant Jeff McBain had seen all of the bad parts. But being the experienced sports dad that he was — and having been a college football player himself — he knew enough not to say anything about the game until Ben did, which wasn't until they were ten minutes into the ride home.

Up until then, the car had been as quiet as the school library.

"Nobody picks me like that," Ben said from the backseat, "even when I go up against older kids in the park."

They were at a stop sign. Ben's dad turned around, grinning. "Now I know that wasn't *technically* a question," he said. "But am I allowed to answer, anyway?"

"Dad, there's not much to say about what you just saw. What everybody just saw."

"Though, I have to say, you have been doing an excellent job yourself *not* saying anything about it," his dad said.

"Please don't give me a pep talk, Dad, I'm begging you," Ben said. "Pep talks are supposed to be before the game, anyway."

"Not always."

"So there's nothing I can do to stop you?"

"Not really, no."

"I was afraid of that," Ben said.

"I just thought I might be able to bring a little perspective," his dad said. "Dads have to at least try. It's a rule they passed for us a while back."

Ben waited.

His dad was driving again, eyes on the road as he said, "You just finished the season of your life in football. And even though you think football season is over now, that you've already moved on, that's not the way it works. Guess what? You and Sam and Coop and the guys, you *haven't* moved on yet, even though you think you have. And by the way? I wouldn't have been able to move on yet, either."

"It's been two weeks," Ben said. "A full week of basketball practice. I'm not using football as an excuse. You know me, Dad. I don't make excuses when I lose."

"But sometimes I *do*," Jeff McBain said. "Think of it as me pulling rank on you."

"I don't even know what that means."

His dad laughed. "It means that I'm the dad and you're the

kid and I get to make the rules, at least sometimes. In the army they'd say that means I outrank you."

"Got it."

"Your body might have been out there on the court today," his dad said, "but I don't believe your brain was. Trust me on this, I'm practically like a brain *surgeon* when it comes to sports."

Ben said, "It wasn't my brain that kept getting beat by that guy today."

"One scrimmage," his dad said. "Which you played *half* of."

"It still felt like a total beatdown to me," Ben said. "A complete facial."

It was how Marv Albert, one of Ben's favorite basketball announcers, described dunks sometimes. The guy dunking the ball giving the guy he was dunking *on* a facial.

"I'm sorry," Ben's dad said. "I know the redheaded kid had a terrific game, but for the life of me I can't remember him throwing one down on you."

"Well, that's the way it felt," Ben said.

He leaned back, closed his eyes. But it wasn't like the ride over to Darby now, this time when he closed his eyes, there were no sweet memories from the championship game in football.

Just one picture after another of Chase Braggs scalding him. All day long.

"I am gonna have to get a whole lot better," Ben said finally, filling one more silence in the car.

"And you will," his dad said.

There was still plenty of daylight left when they got home, even though the afternoon had gotten colder. Ben ran upstairs, threw on a hoodie, grabbed his outdoor basketball, went straight to the hoop at the far end of McBain Field.

Went to work.

Ben had nothing against going out and practicing by himself and trying to get better.

When it was baseball season he had absolutely no problem with asking his dad for the key to the batting cage behind the Y, feeding balls into the machine, working on his swing, making himself take pitch after pitch up the middle if he could, giving himself points every time he'd smack a line drive off the machine.

Ben wasn't afraid of work.

But more than anything, he just wanted to *play*.

He wanted to play games, real games or pickup games with his boys. Even video games. He just loved to compete, that was the real fun of sports for him and why when one season ended he really couldn't wait for the next one to begin.

Only now the next season for him had begun like this, in a glorified pickup game that felt as real as it could possibly be, even an hour after it had ended. Getting scalded and schooled and torched like that by the new guy.

It was why he was out here at McBain Field, the hoop with the blue halfcourt in front of it, the key and the free-throw line and the lane painted in white, even though all the paint was beginning to fade and Ben had noticed that there were even a few more little potholes than he'd noticed the last time he had been out here shooting around.

When Ben was on his way out the door his dad had said, "I assume you're gonna be out there awhile, right?"

Ben nodded.

"Till dinner?" his dad said.

"At least."

"Have at it."

"Don't worry," Ben said. "I will."

He didn't need to warm up, mostly because he was still hot from the game.

It was the steals Chase Braggs had made against him that bothered him more than anything.

If there was one thing Ben was most proud of in basket-ball, it was the way he could handle the ball, even with small hands. He could handle and he could dribble with *both* hands, even at eleven. His dad had always told him that being able to dribble with both hands in basketball was like being a switch-hitter in baseball.

One of Ben's first coaches in the Y league, fourth grade, Mr. Russell, had said to him: "The way to play this game as a point guard is not let the guy guarding you *over*play."

So even though Ben was right-handed he'd never cared if somebody tried to force him to go left, because he *had* a left hand, and wasn't afraid to use it. It was why he'd always been able to drive the defense crazy because they didn't know which hand he was going to use when he wanted to drive to the basket.

Until today, anyway.

Today Chase Braggs had been able to read him like Ben was his favorite book. Like he knew where Ben was going before Ben did. Even though they'd never set eyes on each other before the scrimmage, it seemed as if Chase already knew all of Ben's best moves, as if they had played more games against each other than Bird and Magic did.

It was why the boy who loved to play was out here working, working *hard*, at McBain Field. Thinking to himself how it never really ended in sports, how even though there was always a new season coming along there was always a new challenge, some new way you had to prove yourself.

In football he'd had to prove that he was a better quarterback than Shawn O'Brien, the coach's son, despite the fact that Shawn was so much bigger than Ben, that he looked the part of a quarterback so much more than Ben did.

And, man oh man, he *had* proved it, right through the last play of the championship game, that pass to Sam Brown. Only now here came Chase Braggs, an opponent he had to overcome instead of a teammate like Shawn.

Even though Chase wasn't *all* that much bigger than Ben, his longer arms and greater wingspan just made him seem bigger than he actually was, especially when he was taking the ball away from Ben and making it look so freakishly easy. But it wasn't just the steals. One time he'd backed off at exactly the right moment, right as Ben was committed to passing the ball to Sam on the wing, Chase jumping the route the way cornerbacks in football did when they seemed to just know where the quarterback was going to throw. He had intercepted Ben's pass and almost in the same motion thrown the ball all the way down the court to Ryan Hurley for an easy two.

People always liked to talk about what a great head Ben had for basketball.

Only Chase had been in it all day.

And still was.

It was one of the reasons why Ben didn't even think about shooting the ball the first half hour he was out here. He just dribbled. Side to side, sometimes going all the way around the small court, switching back and forth from his right hand to his left, changing direction sometimes on the fly, crossing over, keeping the ball low. Imagining Chase on him, ready to swipe at the ball with those long arms, Ben making sure to keep his free arm up, the free arm and his body between the imaginary defender and the ball.

Going back to basics.

Basketball 101.

One week before the start of the real season for the Rockwell Rams.

"It was just one lousy scrimmage," Coop had said when it was over.

But Ben knew better. He had seen something today, found out something about his own game at the same time he'd gotten a good look at Chase's for the first time.

He *had* to get better, because he was going to see Chase Braggs a lot. Three regular-season games, the first next Saturday. And then, if Rockwell and Darby managed to finish 1–2 in the league, again in the championship game.

Which right now seemed as far away as the moon he could see now in the sky.

He took a quick break now, knowing he'd start to run out of daylight soon. Running back to the house, getting a couple of the plastic stick figures his dad had brought home from the Y one time. They were the kind of stick figures you saw in parking lots and even in the street sometimes, reminding everybody that there were children in the area and to drive slowly.

There had been a delivery of them to the Y, more than Jeff McBain needed there. So he'd brought some of the extras home, telling Ben they were perfect to use when he wanted to practice his passing when his friends weren't around.

Ben carried four of them back to the court, spread them around, started hitting them with passes off the dribble. Not minding when he'd miss and have to go chase the ball, it just made him more determined to make a sharper, better pass next time.

Ben making sure he didn't telegraph passes to the orange stick figures the way he had when Chase had been guarding him during the game.

As easy as it would have been to just write it off as one bad day, one lousy scrimmage, Ben knew in his heart that he had looked as bad as he had because Chase was that *good*.

Starting to get darker now. Close to dinner. Ben shooting the ball now. Step-back moves and drives to the basket and the little teardrop floater he liked to use when he had to get the ball up and over taller guys in the lane. He fell once as he went down the baseline, stepping in a hole he didn't see, skinned his knee, got right back up. What did they always tell you in sports? No pain, no gain. Every once in a while he'd stop and do one of his favorite basketball things, at least out here: Make free throws underhand. Ben's favorite basketball movie was *Hoosiers*, nothing else even close, and he loved the scene where the guy Ollie made his two big free throws underhand, winning a game for Hickory High with three seconds left on the clock.

Not so long after he saw somebody shoot them that way in the movie, Ben and his dad were watching ESPN Classic, watching an old-time player named Rick Barry, and when Ben saw him shoot free throws *under*hand, he'd said, "I thought only the guys as old as dinosaurs shot like that."

"Not only did Rick Barry shoot them that way," his dad had said, "he was pretty much the best free-throw shooter I ever saw."

"Then how come everybody doesn't shoot them that way?" Ben had said, and his dad said, "Because they don't want to look funny. Or not cool."

Ben had gotten so good at doing it, alone usually, sometimes with Sam in a game of H-O-R-S-E, that he sometimes thought he was better underhand than shooting regulation.

He made ten in a row, then went back to working on his ballhandling, what he was really out here for, Saturday afternoon becoming Saturday night, the air *much* cooler, but Ben sweating now like he'd been running end-to-end drills in an overheated gym.

"I feel like I'm out of breath just watching you."

Ben's head whipped around, but he already knew the voice, knew it was Lily.

"You shouldn't sneak up on people like that, you know," he said.

"A police car with its siren blaring could have snuck up on you, McBain."

"Just practicing, is all."

"That what you call it?"

She had arrived — quietly — on her bike. Wearing jeans and the Packers T-shirt he'd gotten her after Aaron Rodgers, his favorite football player in the world, had beaten the Steelers in the Super Bowl played at Cowboys Stadium. Ben saw she had on her new white Pumas with the pink stripe. When he'd asked why pink she'd said, "Because as good as I am at hanging with boys, I'm still a girl."

Boy, was she ever a girl.

Now Lily said, "I've never seen one-on-*none* basketball look like a contact sport before."

"Don't know what you're talking about, Lils."

"Really?"

"Really" with Lily, in that tone of voice, a certain look on her face, was the same as her calling him a liar. In a nice way, of course.

"Just out here trying to get better," Ben said.

"Better than who, Kobe and LeBron?"

Before Ben could say anything to that, Lily hit him with this: "I heard about the scrimmage, McBain. And about the way Chase played. And the way *you* played. Or didn't."

"Don't want to talk about it right now," Ben said.

Now Lily smiled at him, like the first light coming on in the neighborhood tonight, and said, *"Really?"*

"I give up."

Lily said, "That's always best."

They sat down on the court. Ben told her his version of the scrimmage, how good *he* thought Chase was, how he — Ben — didn't want to wait until tomorrow to get after it, and get better.

"You're always trying to get better," Lily said. "Because that gives you a better chance of winning the game."

"That's the thing, Lils. I had no chance to win the game today."

"Wow," she said. "I didn't know you'd taken on Darby all by yourself. That hardly seems fair."

"Not what I meant."

"Sounded that way to me. Let me ask you something: If you'd played your absolute best game today, would you guys have won?"

Ben was tired all of a sudden. Tired from the game, tired

31

from his postgame practice. Tired of talking already, even with Lily, even knowing she wanted him to feel better. Ben looked past her, across the street to where his house was. How come your parents never called you when you wanted them to?

Like right now.

"Probably not," he said. "They're pretty good. Darby, I mean. I would've picked us to win the league, but that was before they got Chase."

"Which is why you're gonna practice until it's too dark. Or maybe until next Saturday's game."

"I'm done now."

"You think Sam and Coop and Shawn, all your boys, were so freaked by the scrimmage that they gave themselves basketball detentions?"

"It's my job to make the other guys on the team better," Ben said.

"Your *job*?"

"You know me better than anybody," Ben said. "So you know what I mean."

"I know you gotta chill, McBain. Aren't you the guy always telling me that you're never as bad as you look when you lose, and never as good as you look when you win?"

"Have you forgotten anything I've ever said?"

Lily smiled again. "Oh, sure. I try to forget your dumb jokes, how your fantasy teams are doing. Lots of neat stuff. You want the whole list?"

"No, thank you."

Ben could hear his mom calling him now, seeing Lily with him and asking if she wanted to stay for dinner, Lily yelling back that she had to go, she and her parents were going out tonight.

"Here's the deal," Ben said. "I just got the earliest wake-up call I've ever gotten on a season today. I gotta find a way to get better. Fast."

"Or what?" she said in a quiet voice, those eyes of hers on him.

"Or else we're not going to win the championship," he said.

Lily shook her head, stood up. "What, now every season has to end the way the football one did?"

"Why not?"

"Why *not*?" Lily said. "Because that's not the way things work in sports. Not even for you, McBain."

Lily told him he better go get something to eat, lack of food was clearly making him light-headed. Then she got on her bike and said she'd call him later, when he was making more sense.

Ben picked up his ball, drove to the basket one last time. But right before he was going to push off on his left foot, he dribbled the ball into one more hole he didn't see and it bounced away from him.

He thought: End of a perfect day.

The schedule during the season was for their team to practice three nights during the week, an hour at a time at either Rockwell Middle School or at Rockwell High School, the practices only an hour because so many other town teams used the gyms, too.

But even on days when there wasn't practice, Ben was out on the court at McBain, getting ready for the start of the season this Saturday.

Friday afternoon after school, no practice scheduled that night, Ben even got Sam to come work out with him.

Sam Brown wasn't as good an all-around basketball player as Chase Braggs, not based on what they all saw in the first scrimmage. But he had been the quickest and fastest small forward in the league last season, even though he wasn't really small, he was tall enough to play center for the Rams. But Coach just thought Sam's skills still fit small forward best:

He could run the court, he could cover, and his outside shot had gotten a lot better over the summer.

But as far as Ben was concerned, the best part of his friend's game was how unselfish he was. Ben knew Sam well enough to know that he didn't give a rip what his stats were at the end of the game as long as their team won.

Sam wasn't just a good defender, he was an awesome defender, taking pride in locking down the player he was guarding, using *his* long arms and length on defense to his advantage the way Chase did.

Because of all that, Ben decided Sam was the perfect guy to go up against in one-on-one as a way of getting ready for Darby.

Which meant getting ready for his rematch with Chase.

"You usually hate playing one-on-one," Sam was saying now.

"There's a reason."

"Can't wait to hear this one."

"The *reason*," Ben said, "is that even as competitive as you know I am —"

"You? Competitive?"

Ben ignored him. "As I was saying, even as competitive as I am, I don't like to compete against *you*. Guys think I always want us to be on the same team in everything because it gives us a better chance to win. That's not it. I just don't want to beat you. That make sense?"

"Actually it does," Sam said. "It's why I don't like to play video games against my dad. I act like I want to beat him, but I really don't."

"Same."

"But you want me to go at you hard today, right?" Sam said.

"Yeah," Ben said. "At first I wanted to go two-on-two, but Shawn had a guitar lesson and Coop had to stay after school for not getting his English paper in on time. Then I got to thinking about it, and the stuff I still need to work on, it's better with just you and me."

Sam said, "I always look at it the same way: When you get better, the team gets better."

"Let's hope," Ben said.

Ben figured that if he could get his shot against Sam today, he could get it against Chase tomorrow in a game that counted. If he could protect the ball against Sam's long arms and stupidly quick hands, well, he could do that against Chase.

That was the plan, anyway.

"Before we start, can I ask you something?" Sam said. "Why are you so fixed on a dude you'd never even met until last weekend?"

"You sound like Lily."

"Thank you," Sam said. "But is that your answer?"

"Okay, here's the way I look at it," Ben said. "If I'm gonna be as good as I want to be and we're gonna be as good as we need to be, I can't let this guy dominate me. Is *that* a good enough answer?"

"You left one thing out."

"What?"

"How much he annoyed you while he was dominating you."

Sam took the ball out of Ben's hands, turned and squared up, and made a shot from the free-throw line. Then, as he jogged over to pick up the ball, he bobbed his head and smiled and pointed into an imaginary crowd.

Then he blew a kiss at Ben, even though Chase hadn't done *that* last Saturday.

"You *sure* he didn't annoy you?" Sam said.

"Maybe a little bit."

"Maybe a lot."

Ben said, "Are we gonna play or talk?"

Sam said, "Coop thinks you're always supposed to do both."

"Coop's being kept after school."

"I feel like I am, too," Sam said, then grinned and added, "Just kidding."

Today Ben actually tried to beat Sam at one-on-one, pretending as well as he could that he really was going up against Chase. And kept telling Sam to play his hardest, not go easy on him.

"Just worry about yourself," Sam said. "You're the one on a mission here."

"Yeah, to kick your butt."

"If you can."

They played two games of first-to-eleven, only had to win by one. Sam won the first, Ben won the second. Both by a single basket. When Ben would get careless with the ball, Sam would knock it away from him. When Ben didn't make a good enough move or create enough separation between him and Sam, Sam would block his shot. One time Ben had him clearly beaten off the dribble, drove to the basket on the right side, and Sam still managed to come from behind and block the shot, hard, knocking it all the way into the street.

When Ben retrieved it, Sam said, "Listen, when you go up against bigger guys —"

"You mean when I go up against almost everybody," Ben said.

"— you should think about shooting the ball on the way up. Or even *before* you go up, which means before the defense expects it."

So they practiced that for a few minutes, Ben releasing his shot close to the basket before his feet left the ground, working on shooting it from his hip almost as the ball came up out of his dribble, like it was all one motion.

"One more game," he said finally.

"Do I get a vote?" Sam said.

"No."

"Wait, *no* was my vote!"

Ben shrugged as Sam said, "Coop's right, this isn't much of a democracy around here."

"C'mon," Ben said, "you're making me get better."

"All you're doing is making *me* tired."

"You never get tired."

"No, that's you."

"One more game of eleven."

"Seven."

"Deal."

They got to 6–all. Sam's ball. He started backing in, patiently trying to get to his spot in the low blocks, because they'd both seen last Saturday that was one of Chase's go-to moves against Ben, a way to use his length. But this time Sam turned and the ball hit hard off the back of the rim and Ben chased down the rebound, dribbled outside, Sam not giving him any space, running with him.

But Ben went to his left hand, got a step, got into the lane. Only instead of driving the ball all the way, trying to get a layup, he went with the from-the-hip shot he'd been working on, shooting the ball off his right foot instead of his left, a pretty little teardrop.

Nothing but string.

He and Sam bumped fists and Sam said, "Want to blow me a kiss?"

"That's not me."

Sam gave him a long look now. "Nope, definitely not you these days."

"What's that mean?"

"I'm just playing with you," Sam said.

"Seriously?" Ben said.

"That's it!" Sam said. "You cracked the code. You're playing way too seriously."

"I just want to have a good season," Ben said, "is all."

"We all do," Sam Brown said. "It's just that the rest of us have sort of figured out that the season hasn't started yet."

"Well, it *already* started for me," Ben said.

"You're *joking*. I hadn't picked up on that. Coop, either. Or Shawn. Or Lily."

"Go ahead, have your fun."

"You first," Sam said.

The Rams had had a good week of practice, offense and defense, running their plays, getting better at pressing and breaking a press, working hard on being the kind of help defenders that Coach Wright wanted them to be, learning when to switch and when not to, and when he wanted them to double-team the ball.

Ben could see them coming together as a team. More than anything, Ben could see how much Shawn was going to help them this season. Shawn's dad had played in the NFL as a backup quarterback to Peyton Manning, and had raised Shawn to be a quarterback before things had changed halfway through the football season, but Ben was starting to think basketball might be Shawn's best sport.

Starting to think Shawn had no idea just how good a basketball player he might turn out to be.

Shawn could run the court almost as well as Sam and was a better outside shooter, even playing power forward. And he was turning out to be a maniac on the boards, rebounding the ball at both ends of the court, another reason why Ben was sure that Shawn, Sam, Coop were going to make up the best front line in their league.

Sam was still the one player on the team Ben knew they could least afford to lose, just because he did so many things well. But it was clear already that Shawn had it in him to be a game changer, too.

Ben was trying to be one now against Darby. Holding their own this time, even though they were behind eight points at halftime. The Rams had gotten behind by more than that early, Chase and his teammates coming out hot again in the first quarter, same as they had last Saturday in their gym.

But then Darrelle, the Rams' shooting guard, made a couple of three-pointers, and with two minutes left in the first quarter, the game was tied, and stayed tied until Chase Braggs went on an 8–0 run all by himself at the end of the half, the last coming after he blocked Ben's shot, pushed the ball with time running out, had to pull up at the free-throw line for the jumper that beat the horn and made the score 32–24 for Darby at the half.

Ben went hard after Chase, had no chance to catch up, watched from the top of the key as he buried the jumper. Then walked over toward the Rams' bench, slapping his thigh hard with his right hand.

"I should have passed it to you," Ben said.

"No," Shawn said. "Baby jumper, right side, we'd want you taking that every time."

"Chase seemed pretty happy with my shot selection," Ben said.

Coop said, "Dude, that's the only shot of yours he got the whole half. No worries, we got this today."

"You know how much it always chafes me to say this," Sam said, "but Coop's right. We showed that we can play with those guys. And with *that* guy."

After they'd all gotten their drinks, Coach Wright talked about all the good things he'd seen from them, starting with the way they'd fought back after another bad start. Then he went through his personal checklist, all the things he stressed at practice, about sharing the ball, focusing on their next stop.

"We could've folded up like a cheap suit," Coach said, and Ben could see Sam and Coop smiling at him.

Coach had a colorful way of talking. They were studying metaphors in English right now, and Ben knew enough about them to know that Coach was constantly mixing his. The other day he had been talking about a game he'd been watching on television and said he got interested even though he didn't have a horse in that fight.

"But we didn't fold," Coach continued, "and that's why I'm now seeing the team I expect us to be. Just keep playing hard and having fun." Smiling up at them as he said, "Which are one and the same as far as I'm concerned."

As they went out to start the second half, Sam leaned close to Ben and said, "Where did Coach get a crazy idea like that, having fun against the hated Chase?"

Ben said, "I don't hate Chase."

Shawn was behind them. "Well I'm starting to hate him. The

guy doesn't let you get comfortable on defense for a second. It's like he can see everything, even when he's looking the other way."

"Let's just have him see us get a W," Ben said. "See how comfortable he is with that."

"I hear *that*," Shawn said.

It was 47–41, Darby, at the end of the third. Both coaches had done a lot of substituting in the quarter, both making sure everybody on their teams got to play. But when they went out to start the fourth quarter, Ben could see the Darby coach, Mr. Coppo, going with his starters, same as the Rams were.

Rams ball, side out, Chase next to Ben on the court, waiting for the ref to hand the ball to Darrelle.

"Well, now it's on," Chase said.

Ben didn't respond.

"Don't want to talk?" Chase said.

"After the game," Ben said.

Chase gave Ben a little pat on his back and said, "Well, if you still want to."

The crowd was a lot bigger this Saturday, maybe because the game did count, and so the noise from the parents seemed to build as the game stayed close, and kept building to what Ben was sure was going to be a great ending.

Wanting to make sure it was the right one for the Rams.

There was even a moment, Shawn and Darby's Ryan Hurley on the ground fighting for a loose ball, when Ben thought they might really go at it, neither one of them willing to take his hands off the ball. But Sam and Coop pulled Shawn up and away from Ryan — Shawn having finally ripped the ball away — before things turned stupid.

Shawn, breathing hard, said, "We are *totally* coming away with the W."

Darby led by a point, 57–56, with a minute left. Down the stretch, Chase had seemed perfectly willing to pass the ball every time the Rams tried to collapse on him, had only taken two shots that Ben could remember the whole fourth quarter, making both of them.

But now, at the Rockwell end, Sam lost his man on a switch, Ben threw him a perfect bounce pass, Sam made a jumper from the right corner. The Rams were ahead, 58–57. First lead of the game for them, first lead of the new season.

Chase came right back, came right at Sam, got a step, seemed to slow down like he was about to pass again, got Shawn — who'd jumped out on him — to relax just enough before Chase blew past him for a layup.

For most of the game, it seemed to Ben as if the guy had kept his showboating to a minimum. He still found ways to draw attention to himself, like he couldn't help it. He'd just been less annoying so far today.

Even if he was still annoyingly good.

But now it all seemed to kick back in for him, he took a wide route back on defense so he could slap Mr. Coppo a low five, then pointed with both index fingers at his parents.

Forty seconds left, Darby back up by a point.

Ben held up a fist as he brought the ball up. It wasn't a play so much as a trigger, his sign to Sam to come up to the top of the key for a high pick-and-roll. Not a set play as much as the outline for one. But always the best way for them to get into their offense, Coach Wright trusting Ben enough to let him decide where the play should go, what they had, once Sam set his pick.

Sam set a beauty now and, as soon as he did, Chase yelled, "Switch!" and jumped out on him. Sam still knew enough to run around him and then cut toward the basket, Chase backing up with him, watching Ben's eyes as he did.

And Ben purposely kept his eyes on Sam as he kept dribbling, waiting until Shawn came around the pick Coop had set for him on the baseline. When Shawn cleared the pick, Ben fired a pass to him and watched as Shawn turned and made a short, no-sweat jumper, like he was still shooting around during pregame warm-ups.

Rockwell by a point, twenty seconds left, the gym louder than it had been all afternoon, everybody on their feet, Mr. Coppo making no move to get up or call a time-out, putting the game in Chase's hands.

Letting his guys play.

Ben picked up Chase in the backcourt, trying to get him to burn a few extra seconds having to deal with Ben, hoping to make him rush a little once he got the ball past midcourt. But Chase spun away from him, pushed the ball hard up the sideline, Ben scrambling to get in front of him.

Seeing Chase smiling as he did.

Like he'd waited all day to get *here*.

Ben saw Chase's eyes go to the clock. Ben followed his gaze.

Fifteen seconds.

Chase waved his left arm now, telling his teammates to clear out. So it was him against Ben.

Ten seconds now.

Chase started backing him in then. The way Ben had told Sam to back him in at McBain the day before. Still not rushing, taking his time, not looking for a clock himself. Like the clock was one more thing he could see without looking.

Backing Ben toward the low blocks.

Ben tried to reach around him for the ball, but didn't come close, Chase blocking him with his free arm just as he went into his shot, turning and shooting in one motion, falling away just slightly, putting up the soft jumper that won the first game of the season for Darby.

This time Chase didn't just hold his shooting pose, he turned with his right hand high and pointed at the scoreboard:

Visitor 61, Home 60.

And even as his teammates ran for him, Chase still wasn't quite done. Almost like he'd left himself just enough time to get off one more shot, not over Ben this time, but right in his face.

Taking a long step forward, smiling that cocky smile, leaning down so that only Ben could hear, saying:

"You actually think you can stop me, little man?"

# 7

Lily had been at the game, and when it was over she told Ben they needed to walk into town for ice cream, Lily Wyatt always believing that ice cream could cure just about anything wrong in your world, or the whole world.

"What if I said I didn't want any company right now, *or* ice cream?" Ben said.

"You'd be wrong," Lily said. "You know you want both."

Sam and Coop and Shawn and the rest of the players were tearing into the snacks that Mrs. Manley had brought, cookies and brownies and chips and Gatorade. Ben and Lily were sitting at the top of the bleachers, just the two of them.

Chase and the Darby players were already gone, even though the scoreboard was still lit, still had the final score on it.

"I really don't feel like it," Ben said.

"Well, now you're just being plain old silly."

Coop yelled up from the court that he and Sam were going to Shawn's house to play video games, maybe throw a football around on the cool turf field his dad had built for him behind their house. Ben told them to go ahead, maybe he'd check them later, for now he was going to hang with Lily.

"See how easy that was?" Lily said.

"Let me just go tell my parents we're going into town."

Lily said, "I already did."

When they were outside, Ben told Lily what Chase had said to him after making his shot to win the game.

"You believe that?" he said.

"Oh, it doesn't sound so terrible to me," she said. "You make it sound like he stole your bike or something."

"You're joking, right?"

"You know how guys trash-talk each other during games." She pounded her chest a couple of times and then in a deep, caveman voice she said, "Me good. You bad."

Ben said, "You're telling me you think it's okay?"

"Well, as okay as boys being boys can ever be."

Smiling as she did.

"I don't recall you ever acting like that when you scored a game-winning goal in soccer."

"But you know what?" Lily said, "I want to sometimes. You're. telling me that you never do?"

"I might want to," Ben said, "but I never do."

It was only a short walk from Rockwell Middle School into town. They were passing the YMCA now, Ben feeling a sudden urge to tell Lily he'd decided to pass on getting ice cream after all, wanting to go inside his dad's Y and see if there was a free basket in one of the gyms.

Instead he said to her, "No matter how much I might want to pound my chest when my team wins, I don't. C'mon,

Lils, you know that's not the way I think you're supposed to act."

"But, see, that's the thing, not everybody thinks the same way you do," Lily said. "And I gotta tell you, McBain, it would be pretty boring if they did."

"Now I'm boring?"

"Nope. Maybe a tad sensitive, I'm thinking. Never boring. And neither is Chase."

"What's Chase got to do with this?"

"Practically everything?" Lily said.

"Are you asking or telling?" Ben asked. "Sometimes it's hard to tell with you."

"Hey, I just think he's fun to watch," she said. "Remember, when I first heard about him, I thought he sounded like he might be a pretty cool rival for you. And that was *before* I saw him play. Now that I *have* seen him play, I'm *positive* he's going to be a totally cool rival for you."

Ben said, "So I'm boring and he's cool and fun. Got it."

"Now you really are being silly," Lily said. "I'm just saying that the two of you going up against each other this season can be cool and fun. Mostly because you're so different. Like when you got me to watch that movie about Bird and Magic, that's what I came away with, how different they were, and not just because of the way they played. Magic was all smiles all the time and Larry Bird, he was so serious you wondered if he *ever* smiled."

Ben made a motion like he was checking something off an invisible list.

"Check," he said. "I'm also too serious."

Lily poked him with her elbow so he could see her smiling at him again. "Usually? No. Lately. *Yes!*"

Ben said, "I can't believe you like that guy."

"I *like* watching him play," she said. "I like watching you play. And I'm not gonna lie to you, Big Ben, but I can't wait until the next time you two play against each other." She put out her hands, like he was going to cuff her, said, "There, I've confessed, take me away, Officer."

Ben didn't want a rematch with Chase right now. But he did want to be playing. Alone. On the court at McBain. Wanted that more than ice cream, more than being with Lily. But he knew if he told her that, she'd start in all over again about him being too serious.

When she thought he was acting like that, she called him the king of the non-smilers.

Ben said, "I'm glad you find this all so hilarious."

"Oh, lighten up, McBain," she said, "you know I'm not really busting on you."

"Glad we cleared *that* up."

Lily said, "Do you want my honest opinion about Chase?"

Back to Chase. It was as if he were going for ice cream with them.

"Do I have a choice?" Ben said.

Lily said, "I honestly think you should look at him as a fun challenge, and *not* act like even the idea of playing against him is worse than having your TV privileges taken away."

Ben didn't say anything right away, both of them waiting for the light to change at the corner of Main and Elm, and so Lily finally said, "Well?"

"You're right," he said.

"You're kidding."

"Nope, Lils, you *are* right. So thank you."

"Just doing my job."

He didn't think she was right. Not even close. He couldn't believe *Lily* — of all people — didn't believe the guy was out of line for chirping on Ben after the game. Couldn't believe she thought this hot dog was fun to watch. But he knew that if he didn't drop the subject, drop it right now, she was going to think he was even more fixed on Chase. Or more sensitive on the subject than she already thought he was. Basically Ben just wanted the conversation to be over now. So he ended it in a way that had always worked for him in the past. Or almost always worked. Ben's dad joked sometimes, even in front of Ben's mom, that the most important words in the English language for any guy were these:

"You're right, dear."

"I gotta chill on Chase or it's going to be a long season." Ben said.

They crossed Main Street and walked through the door to Two Scoops, sat down at the counter, and both ordered banana splits, Lily announcing that there would be no more talk about Chase Braggs or the Rockwell-Darby game for the rest of the afternoon.

But while they waited for their ice cream, Ben was still thinking about Chase. Thinking that it really was like the guy had made the walk into town with them, almost like they should have ordered something for him.

It wasn't enough that Chase had made the shot. Or that

his team had won because of it. Or that even when the game was over he was still talking.

No.

Now on top of all that, there was something just as bad.

Maybe worse.

Lily thought the guy was cool.

Lily walked Ben all the way home, even though her own house was on the way and she knew she'd have to double-back later.

Before she left Ben, the two of them standing on the sidewalk at the end of his brick walk, she said, "Pretty quiet, McBain."

"Talked out," he said, almost adding something about how Lily probably couldn't understand that, since she *never* seemed to get talked out.

But he didn't. Because he really *was* talked out.

Lily said, "You sure that's all it is?"

"Lils," he said, "I already told you that you were right, I'm gonna change my attitude. Big-time. Go back to having fun, remind myself that the fun of any season is finding out how it's going to come out."

"So you're not mad at me?"

"Who said I was mad at anybody?"

"You didn't exactly act happy when I told you I didn't think Chase was some kind of grand master dweeb dorkmeister."

53

"Dweeb dorkmeister?"

"These ideas just come to me sometimes, I can't control them."

Ben smiled at her. "Try harder. And, no, I don't expect you to be hating on Chase."

"Even though you are?" she said. Smiling back.

Ben grabbed his head in mock pain, saying, "Why are we still talking about this?"

"Okay, we're done now," Lily Wyatt said, and laughed, and started running down Ben's street, past McBain Field, not looking back.

Boy oh boy.

*What* a girl.

Whether you always agreed with her or not.

The next day Sam and Coop and Shawn came over for the big Sunday lunch that was a tradition in the McBain household. Lily had been invited, too, as a member of what they now called the Core Four Plus One, but she had to go to her aunt's house in Darby, before she played one of her last travel soccer games of the year over there.

So it was Ben and his guys and Ben's parents sitting around the big round table in their dining room, the guys doing most of the talking, Ben's mom and dad just taking it all in, smiling a lot, as if this was the only place in the world they wanted to be right now. During the NFL season, Beth McBain always scheduled lunch for noon, in case the Packers — Ben's favorite team in the world, with his favorite player, Aaron Rodgers — were on television at one o'clock.

"It's weird," Coop said when they were having their pie and ice cream for dessert, "that the NFL has only played about half its season so far and we've already started basketball."

"Not sure you can say that about me the way I played yesterday," Ben said. "Maybe my season can start next Saturday."

"Here we go," Sam said, grinning.

"Here what goes?" Ben said.

Sam turned to Coop and Shawn and said, "Like he doesn't know, right?"

Shawn put his head down, went back to work on dessert, grinning as he said, "I'm *so* staying out of this. I'm still like a newbie with you guys."

"Hey, I've been good today," Ben said to Sam, "I haven't brought up yesterday's game one time."

"Which you acted like was more horrible than if the Packers had lost to the Bears."

"Hey, have your fun," Ben said, "but you know that we can't win the championship if we can't beat the *Darby* Bears."

"Hey," Coop said, "they've got to play the season, too. Somebody else could beat them."

"Really?" Ben said.

Coop said, "So we'll have to figure it out, and we've got plenty of time, we don't play them again for a while."

The next time they were playing Darby was in the fifth game of the season, right before the Christmas break in the town basketball schedule. Then the two teams played again in the last game of the regular season. Usually teams in the league only played each other once during the regular season, but Rockwell and Darby had always played each other twice, just because of the rivalry between the two towns. This year they'd added a third game when Fort Stuart decided to join a different league. The kids were fine with it, loving the big crowds they got, almost like they were in training for what Rockwell vs. Darby would be like when they got to high school.

The Game of the Year, times three this year.

One down, two to go.

"Here's the deal," Sam said. "We only lost by a bucket yesterday. You don't think we can figure out a way for us to find those two points before we do play them again?"

"They could get better, too," Ben said.

Not giving ground.

"But you know that we *always* get better, in every sport, as the season goes along," Coop said. "Like we didn't in football?"

"Basketball is different," Ben said. "One guy can make a bigger difference when it's just five on the team."

"Chase is still just one guy," Shawn said.

"So's LeBron," Ben said.

"Whoa," Sam said. "Now Chase Braggs is LeBron *James*?"

"Dad," Ben said, "help me out here."

His dad leaning back in his chair, arms crossed, looking happy, taking it all in.

"Sorry, I'm a football guy," Jeff McBain said.

"Yeah," Ben said, "and you never have any opinions about other sports."

"Well," Ben's dad said, "since you did ask . . . I actually agree with Coop."

"*Yes!*" Coop said, putting his arm up in the air and then pulling it down hard.

Ben's dad said, "You guys always *do* get better as you go. I also agree with Sam. Next time it might be you guys making the last shot, it's not like you got your doors blown off yesterday."

"I'm getting ganged up on here," Ben said. "What about you, Mom? Care to jump in?"

"Guy talk about sports? I'd rather start doing dishes now," she said, both Ben and his dad knowing she was being sarcastic.

"One more thing," his dad said.

"From the football guy," Ben said.

Jeff McBain said, "Not only is your league not just one player, it's not just one team. Who're you guys playing next Saturday?"

"Parkerville," Shawn said.

"Well, my suggestion is to get Chase out of your heads, and replace him with Parkerville."

Looking at Ben as he said that, both of them knowing that he was only worried about what was going on inside his own son's head. But then, it happened that way between them a lot, big father-son talks where his dad had to say hardly anything at all.

*　　*　　*

Shawn and Coop lived on the north side of Rockwell, and had ridden their bikes over to Ben's. After the Packers game ended, they said they were going to head out. Sam said he was going to hang for a while, watch some of the second game of the doubleheader, Cowboys against the Redskins. He said as a Giants' fan it was fun watching Tony Romo throw interceptions.

But then the Cowboys got ahead two touchdowns in the first quarter and scored another halfway through the second. Sam announced that watching the Cowboys win was never any fun for him, and got up to leave.

"Let's go shoot around for a few minutes," Ben said.

"Noooooooo," Sam said. "Can't we have a hoops-free day?"

"Please?" Ben said.

Sam shook his head, already reaching for the ball that was sitting next to the television set. "Sometimes I can't tell what's worse, the way Lily dominates you or the way you dominate me."

You could see it already starting to get dark. Sam said he couldn't believe that Ben hadn't somehow convinced the town council to put lights up at McBain Field, so that Ben could practice like a lunatic as late as he wanted.

"Lunatic? What's so crazy about wanting to see an ending to the basketball season that was like the one we had in football?"

Sam looked past him, squinting, and said, "It's getting too dark out here for me to see anything."

"We don't have to stay out here too long," Ben said.

Sam said, "Where have I heard *that* one before? Wait! I know! *Here!*"

They just took turns shooting around at first, Ben not wanting Sam to think that he'd just brought him out here to play the part of Chase again. After they were warmed up, they played a game of H-O-R-S-E, even as darkness started to come faster now.

After Sam beat Ben with a left-handed baby hook, he said, "Before it gets pitch-black, is there anything you want to work on before I go?"

"You think that's why I brought you out here?"

"Yes."

"Well, since you were nice enough to offer," Ben said, "show me how I can defend a step-back move like the one he put on me yesterday."

"Don't take this the wrong way," Sam said, "but you're never going to be able to defend a bigger guy with a good step-back. It's that way from sixth-grade ball all the way up to the pros."

"I know that," Ben said. "But I keep thinking that if I time my move right, as he's going into *his* move, I might be able to get a hand on the ball."

"Not unless the guy telegraphs when he's going to turn around and square up."

"Let me at least try," Ben said.

Sam shot three straight turnarounds after backing Ben in, made two of them, Ben never came close to putting his hand on the ball.

Sam said, "The only thing I've noticed when a guy tries to put that move on me, is that sometimes the last dribble before he turns, he might pound the ball a little harder. Maybe you could look for that."

"Why don't I look for it right here, first to five baskets?" Ben said. "Now that I know what I'm supposed to be looking for."

"You can't look for anything now," Sam said. "It's too dark!"

"Best of three baskets, then," Ben said. "Who knows, you might improve your shooting eye."

"How does that work," Sam said, "if you already feel like you're shooting blindfolded?"

Ben said they could shoot for it, but Sam said no, just handed him the ball, and said, "Let's get this over with."

Despite the bad light, Ben made a long one from the outside before Sam was up on him. But then Sam blocked his next shot, gave Ben a little up-fake, drove past him for the easy bucket.

"Game time," Sam said.

"Bring it," Ben said.

Thinking to himself that they were all right, Lily and his buds and his dad, that he *was* supposed to be having fun playing ball, that he had to stop stressing on Chase and one stupid loss. Just let the game and the fun of the game come to him the way it was right now with Sam Brown.

Finally seeing it clearly, even out here in the dark.

He even flipped what Chase had said to him yesterday at the end of the game, saying to Sam now, "You think you can score on me, big boy?"

"Kind of," Sam said.

He started backing Ben in, Ben sure he'd try to win the game with the same step-back move they'd been working on, Ben ready to make his own move at exactly the right moment, waiting for Sam to pound that last dribble before he turned.

But when he did, and Ben flashed in for the ball, Sam completely faked him out, laughing as he did, like this was too easy, spun around to a left-hand dribble, completely dusted Ben as he drove in for the easy layup that would win the game.

Until one stride from the basket he stepped in a hole at McBain that neither of them could have seen, his left leg buckling underneath him, Sam going down hard, yelling in a way Ben had never heard Sam Brown yell in his life.

Rolling around on the ground immediately, holding on to his left ankle.

Ben didn't need much light at all to see the pain in Sam's face, hear it in his voice.

"Rolled it bad," he said.

"Don't move," Ben said, "I'll go get my dad."

Sam said, "Let me see if I can walk on it."

"Sam, please wait, I don't want you to hurt it any worse than you already did."

"C'mon," Sam said, trying to force a smile, "now you be a bro and give me a hand."

Ben did. Sam slowly tried to get to his feet, tried to put some weight on the ankle.

Went right down again.

And in that moment Ben was no longer obsessing about a player on somebody else's team. Just about one of his own teammates, one of the best friends he was ever going to have.

One who shouldn't even have been out here in the dark, one who was only out here because he was such a great friend to Ben, and always had been.

Ben pulled Sam up again. Even though he was much smaller, he told Sam to lean on him as they began to walk toward Ben's house, making their way slowly across the field where they'd had so much fun in their lives.

It wasn't broken.

That was pretty much the only good news once they got Sam to Rockwell Medical for X-rays.

Sam had never broken any bones, neither had Ben. So they couldn't tell whether or not Sam had cracked an ankle bone before they got to the hospital, even Ben's dad and mom weren't sure, telling Sam on the way that sometimes a bad ankle sprain could hurt just as much.

And every time Sam was asked about the ankle he said it hurt a lot.

But only when asked. Because he was Sam, he wasn't saying much at all, not on the way to Rockwell Medical, not while they waited outside the emergency room.

Right before a nurse came out to get Sam, just as Sam's parents arrived, Sam did say to Ben, "Dude, don't tell anybody I screamed like a girl when I went down."

Somehow Ben managed a smile, even though he was sure it had to be the smallest one in history, like he was trying to smile through his friend's pain.

"You got it," Ben said. "And I most definitely won't tell Lily. About your scary-movie scream. Or that you said you sounded like a girly girl. If I do, she might do something to your good ankle."

Another nurse came out with a wheelchair, even though Sam said he didn't need one. But the second nurse said it was a hospital rule, helped Sam get out of the chair he'd been sitting in, get into the wheelchair. Ben saw him make a face, dropping his guard for just a second, Ben seeing how much pain his friend was in.

Ben walked alongside him as the nurse pushed the wheelchair across the waiting room.

"I'll be fine," Sam said to Ben.

"Yeah."

"For real."

"Yeah."

Then Sam was through the double doors and gone and, when he finally came back, Ben feeling his heart drop like a rock when he saw Sam on crutches, he found out that Sam Brown wasn't fine at all, at least not for now, and not for a while.

It was a Grade III high ankle sprain, the worst kind, the doctor explaining to Ben and his parents what he'd explained to Sam and *his* parents inside: That there had been a partial tear of the ligament connecting two ankle bones, the fibula and tibia. The two bones having separated, but not broken.

According to the doctor, Sam wouldn't even be able to

start physical therapy for three weeks, the doctor saying that the swelling hopefully would have gone down by then.

While Sam's dad went to pull their car around to the front of the emergency-room entrance, Sam sat back down next to Ben in the waiting room, his ankle already taped with a thick elastic bandage, Ben thinking the ankle looked so big it was as if they'd wrapped the bandage around a basketball.

Just the two of them, Ben's parents talking with Mrs. Brown on the other side of the room.

"How long?" Ben said, both of them knowing exactly what he meant.

Basketball. How long until he could play basketball? Sam Brown's favorite sport. Always his favorite season.

He took a deep breath, let it out, said, "Not until after New Year's, at the earliest." Took another breath, deeper than before, and said, "Dude, I'm not gonna lie, the doctor said if this thing heals slowly, 'cause some do, I might be gone for the season."

"You're faster than anybody I know," Ben said, his voice too loud in the quiet room. "So you'll heal faster than anybody, right?"

"Sounds like a plan to me," Sam said.

"Not just a plan," Ben said to his friend. "Think of it as an order."

Then, for what felt like the hundredth time since Sam had stepped in the hole on his way to the basket, Ben said to him, "I am *so* sorry."

Sam said, "You gotta stop. It was nobody's fault."

Nobody's except mine, Ben thought.

He went straight to his room when he got home, his mom saying she'd make him a sandwich since they'd all missed dinner, Ben telling her he wasn't hungry, his mom saying that he had to eat something.

Ben knew you couldn't win that one even if you had a whole army on your side, so he just thanked her and said that she could call him when it was ready.

When he heard the knock on the door about five minutes later, he thought it was her.

His dad instead.

"Time to eat?" he said.

"Your mother decided to fire up some burgers," Jeff McBain said. "She's under the impression that a hot meal will make you feel better."

"She's wrong," Ben said.

"You want to be the one to tell her?" his dad said, and came in and sat down on his bed and didn't even wait, got right into it, saying, "I'm going to say this one time and then, I promise, I'm not going to say it again: It was an accident, son. On a court I should have fixed up myself if the town didn't want to do it, because I know how much time you spend pounding a ball out there."

"Dad, stop," Ben said. "You didn't do this." Turning around in the swivel chair at his desk, closing the screen on his laptop, where he'd just Googled high ankle sprains. "You didn't do this. I did."

"No one did."

"He didn't even want to play today," Ben said.

Stopping then, feeling the tears he'd been carrying around inside himself coming up strong now.

He swallowed. Hard. Said, "Sam wanted to quit way before it happened."

"He was out there for you the way you would have been out there for him," Jeff McBain said.

What came out of Ben next came out hot.

"It should have been me getting hurt!" he said. "It should have been me out for the stupid season!"

"You don't know that Sam's out for the season and neither does he. And neither does the doctor."

"Well, it sounded that way to me," Ben said.

He stopped again, the tears getting closer now, Ben fighting them again, knowing he would only feel worse if he started crying, that he'd just feel more helpless — and sad — about what had happened to Sam tonight than he already did.

"You know why this is on me?" Ben said. "Because I got so caught up in what I wanted, what I thought I needed to do, I didn't think about anybody else. And that's not me."

"Nope," his dad said. "It's not you. Not gonna sugarcoat it, pal, but you did start to lose your way a little bit. But most guys I know, when they get lost, they just keep driving around while they get *more* lost. Just listening to you right now, you corrected things a lot faster."

He patted the bed, motioned for Ben to come sit next to him, which he did now.

"Yeah," Ben said, "good for me. It took losing Sam for me not to be lost anymore."

Jeff McBain put his arm around him, pulled his son closer. Ben let him.

"Okay, so we know how we got here," his dad said. "The important question is where do we go *from* here?"

"I've been thinking hard on that, Dad."

"You're *kidding*! I never would've known."

"You're not making me laugh," Ben said. "Not tonight."

"I can't make any promises."

Ben said, "I'm gonna start by being a better teammate than I've ever been."

"Pretty hard for you to be a better teammate."

"I always tell everybody else it's a team game, and then I started to forget that myself," Ben said. "Got so caught up with this guy Chase I couldn't see past him."

"There's always gonna be a guy like Chase coming along," his dad said. "That's just the way it works in sports. If it's not your school, or your town, it's the next town. Or it happens at the next level. But there's always gonna be new challenges. And maybe when you're in the sixth grade, they can seem bigger than they actually are."

"You're the one always telling me I play older."

"Well, there is that." He turned so he was facing Ben now.

"Listen, I know Sam will handle this great. He already is. But you've got to do the same."

"Whatever the challenge was before, I had Sam to help me," Ben said.

"He'll just do it from the bench now," his dad said.

"And he's gonna see me playing for him now. Every practice, every game. He's always made me better just by being out there. Now I'm gonna make the other guys better even though he's *not* out there."

"Sounds like a plan," his dad said.

"Better be a good one," Ben said, "since Sam is our best player." He paused and said, "Or used to be."

"You gotta stop thinking that way," his dad said. "You really want my two cents? There it is. This happened on my high school football team. Junior year. Our quarterback, guy named Andy Banks, broke his arm in our first game. And I said to our coach, 'What are we going to do without Andy?' And Coach looked at me and said, 'Who's Andy?' It sounded mean when he said it, but then he explained that what he was telling me was that he could only coach the players he had."

They both heard Ben's mom at the bottom of the stairs, telling them the burgers were almost ready.

Ben said, "The only reason Sam was out there tonight was for me. Until he gets back, I'm gonna be out there for him."

"Win one for Sam?" his dad said.

Ben put an elbow in his dad's ribs, said, "If I ever hear you say that again, the next elbow you get will be a lot worse."

"Our secret," Jeff McBain said.

He put out his fist the way Ben's buds did, and Ben gave him some tap.

But, yeah, Ben thought to himself.

Yeah, his dad had nailed this the way he nailed most of the big things.

Win one for Sam.

There were ten players to a team in their league.

There was no official league rule about every player getting a certain amount of playing time in each game, but most coaches tried to get even the guys at the end of their benches on the court for a few minutes every game.

Get them some "burn," as Coop called it.

Ben's dad said that back when he played town ball, there were fifteen players on each team, but they finally decided that was too many. Then it was twelve, and, even then, the coaches said it was way too hard to get all of them in.

Finally they settled on what Coach Wright called a "perfect ten." He knew he was never going to satisfy all of his players, but at least he could scrimmage five-on-five at practice.

Without Sam Brown, the Rockwell Rams were down to nine players. It means they had to add one player who had gotten cut, and even though they knew it would be up to the board members of Rockwell Basketball to decide who would replace Sam, it didn't stop Coach Wright and the guys on the team from making what turned out to be a unanimous selection:

MJ Lau.

He had been the last guy cut from the team this season, the same as he had been the last guy cut last season, his great heart nearly making up for his lack of pure basketball talent again. MJ was the first to tell you that basketball wasn't his best sport. Soccer was, by far, that's why he didn't play football in the fall despite being wide enough to have played in either the offensive or defensive line.

MJ was a fullback in soccer, playing the right side on defense. Ben and his buds normally weren't big soccer guys — other than when Lily ordered them to attend one of her games — but they loved checking out MJ whenever they could because he had a way of making soccer look like *way* more of a contact sport than football, throwing himself around and walking away from just about every game with a uniform full of dirt, and sometimes a face full of dirt as well.

He played basketball pretty much the same way, diving for loose balls, spending more time horizontal, Sam said one time, than vertical. He couldn't shoot and wasn't much of a ball handler, but he could rebound like a madman. And, man oh madman, could he guard. MJ Lau wasn't big on Coach Wright's theory about always knowing where the ball was no matter how closely you were guarding your man. MJ's idea of playing good D was locking on his man and following him all the way to the locker room if he had to.

He committed fouls all over the place, to the point where Ben sometimes felt he should have started scrimmages during the tryouts with three fouls on him already. And he had no game on offense, none. When you passed MJ the ball, he never looked to shoot or drive, just to get rid of it, like he was afraid if he held on to the ball for more than a second, it might explode in his hands.

But if you needed a stop, MJ could get you a stop. You just hoped he could get it without knocking the other guy a couple of rows into the bleachers.

The other guys on the team loved his heart and his attitude and begged Coach Wright to go to the league and let them have eleven players this season, just so MJ wouldn't have to get cut again, and he wouldn't be their teammate until baseball season started.

But now he'd made the team, the board members, unanimous on MJ once they'd heard Coach Wright's pitch. They all knew it wasn't the way anybody ever wanted to make a team, with somebody getting hurt the way Sam had.

But MJ was finally getting a uniform.

Getting all he ever wanted in basketball, which meant a chance to be on the team, and compete.

MJ was replacing Sam Brown, the best all-around player they had, so they all knew he wasn't going to make them better.

But before he showed up for his first practice on the Tuesday night after Sam's injury, Ben was explaining to Coach how they were all going to *feel* better just having MJ in the gym. He was just one of those guys, like Coop. You smiled as soon as you saw him come through the door.

Ben and Coach had been the first to show up at their gym on Tuesday night, sitting high up in the bleachers.

"Glad to hear you say that," Coach Wright said. "Sometimes you find out the hard way that there's all sorts of ways to feel like a winner in sports."

"MJ will help us on D if we can get him not to knock over guys like they're bowling pins," Ben said.

"I want him to do more than that," Coach said. "I want everybody on this team to contribute at both ends."

"Coach, he's not Sam," Ben said, adding, "Mostly because no one is."

"I know that. He's a project. But he's a project who has a chance to be a whole lot better by the end of this season. And the two of us are going to make sure that happens."

Ben lowered his voice, even though nobody was close to them, Coop and Shawn shooting around after having just come through the double doors at the other end of the gym, Sam sitting on the floor under the basket watching them.

"MJ never even played basketball till he tried out last season," Ben said. "Coach, you were there for every minute of the tryouts. He struggles making *layups*. Let's just say that the MJ in his name doesn't stand for Michael Jordan."

His real name was Mark Johnson Lau. Same as his dad's. They didn't want to call him Junior, so he had always been MJ.

"You always make the guys around you better," Coach said. "So make him better."

"Easier said than done sometimes."

"Your teammates take their lead from you," Coach said. "Starting tonight, I just want you to make sure they don't treat

MJ like some kind of mascot. I'm not asking you to turn him into Sam, we both know that's not happening, he's gotta be himself. It's your job to help him find his best self. It's what point guards do."

"You think he can help us on offense for real?"

Coach laughed. "Well, maybe not tonight," he said. "Hey, I know that as fearless as he is, he's also totally afraid of somebody passing him the ball. But like I said, before the season's over, we're gonna change that."

"But I can't remember him scoring a single basketball during *tryouts*," Ben said.

MJ was in the gym now, and even from the other end of the court you had to notice two things: How big his smile was and how white his new sneakers were.

Coach said, "Think how'll cool it will be when he gets one in a real game."

He started to get up, now that most of the Rams seemed to have shown up all at once, but Ben put a hand on his arm and said, "Ask you something?"

"Ask away."

"I hear what you want me to do with MJ," Ben said. "But what are we gonna do without Sam?"

Coach Wright gave Ben a smile as big as the one MJ was still wearing as he ran around the court high-fiving everybody in sight.

"Let's get down there and start finding out," Coach said.

"We can't be as good without Sam as we would have been with him," Ben said.

"I don't know that," Coach said, "and neither do you. It's like an old tennis teacher of mine told me one time when I was about your age: That's why they put the net up."

He stopped and turned and said to Ben, "Trust me: It's gonna be great."

In that moment Ben believed him because he wanted to.

The only legit big guy they had now was Shawn, but as athletic as he was, he was still learning to be a basketball player.

Sam, even playing small forward, had always played like a big, which is what they called "big men" now in basketball. When they went to a zone, Sam was in the middle of it. When the Rams needed a rebound, Sam would go get it. When the other team's center or power forward was its best scorer, it was a no-brainer, Sam would switch over and cover the guy.

And lock him down most of the time.

Last season Ben had never worried about match-up problems, because they had Sam. For the other team, the match-up problem was *him*. Ben had never said anything about this to Sam or anybody else, but when it got down to crunch time against Darby in their opener, he thought Coach might switch Sam over to Chase, just because if you looked at Sam's size and length and quickness, he really matched up a lot better with Chase Braggs than Ben did.

He almost suggested that to Coach, but then his ego wouldn't let him do it. Now it didn't matter. The next time they played Darby, he'd have to figure out a way to lock down Chase himself.

Because Sam was on crutches, sitting next to Coach Wright now because Coach had named him his assistant, watching the Rams play Parkerville without him, seeing what everybody saw once the game started, how much the whole team somehow seemed to have shrunk without him.

Robbie Burnett, the star quarterback of the Parkerville team the Rams had beaten to win the football championship, was also their best — and biggest — player in basketball. Even if he'd only played the second half of last season, missing the first half while he recovered from a broken wrist. On offense he played small forward the same as Sam had, for pretty much the same reasons as far as Ben could tell:

He was a good enough ball handler and good enough passer that it was like having a second point guard on the floor, and playing the position known as the "3" in hoops just gave him more room to operate.

Normally Sam and Robbie would have been guarding each other, the two of them going at each other hard the way they had in a double overtime game last season, the Rams finally winning when Sam somehow got around Robbie on the offensive boards, got a rebound and a put-back one second before they would have gone to overtime number three.

But today Sam could only watch as Robbie did pretty much anything he wanted against Shawn as the Patriots were building a ten-point lead halfway through the second quarter. Shawn couldn't keep up with Robbie outside and when he got inside, Coop couldn't handle him, either. The Rams were playing about as well as they could without Sam on offense, but so far they had no chance on defense.

Ben felt like they were lucky to only be down ten.

So by the time their coach gave Robbie another break, it was 30–20 and Ben was pretty sure without even checking the stat book that Robbie had as many points by himself as the whole Rockwell team.

Maybe Chase Braggs wasn't the best player in the league after all.

At least not today he wasn't.

Coach had given Ben a breather right before Robbie got his, and so he was sitting next to Sam when Coach put MJ Lau on Robbie, to see if MJ could knock him off his game a little bit.

MJ proceeded to foul Robbie three times in about a minute and a half.

Ben said, "This is gonna work great until MJ fouls out."

"Or he puts us in the penalty and Robbie starts shooting free throws," Sam said.

"Whichever comes first," Ben said. "He's gonna drop forty on us the way he's going."

"He'll cool down," Sam said. "Or Coach will figure out a way to slow him down."

"How do you know that?"

Sam grinned. "I don't, actually. I just thought it sounded like something a good assistant coach would say."

"The only chance we've got is if you make a miracle recovery like those people do on TV and you throw down your crutches at halftime."

"I wish," Sam said, and just the way he said it, the way just those two words made you know how much he wanted it to be true, made Ben wish he'd kept his big mouth shut.

"Sorry," Ben said.

"New rules," Sam said. "From now on you have to give me a dollar every time you say 'sorry.' I figure by Christmas, I'll have enough to buy that Xbox 360."

Ben went back out for the last four minutes of the half. The Parkerville coach kept Robbie — who had two fouls — right next to him, playing some guys off their bench.

Over those last four minutes, the Rams played their best ball of the season.

So did Ben McBain.

He fed Shawn for an easy two on a two-on-one break. Then got into the lane for one of his teardrop shots, high over their center, Ben feeling like the ball took about a minute to come down, but hit nothing but string when it did.

Now they were down six.

"Keep pushing it," Coach Wright said as Ben ran past him.

"Copy that," Ben said.

Ben felt himself smiling, feeling it now, maybe for the first time all season. Shawn got a rebound, they pushed it again, Ben drove to the basket, probably had everybody thinking he'd gotten too deep. But what they didn't know was that he'd done it on purpose, one of his favorite moves, went all the way underneath, reached around their center and threw a perfect bounce pass to a cutting Darrelle, money.

The Rams finally got it to 34–32, minute left in the half, Robbie still on the bench, his coach not wanting him to get a third foul before halftime.

Parkerville tried to hold for the last shot, but Ben sneaked in behind their shooting guard, the guy Darrelle was guarding, stole the ball, walked the ball up the court.

Now the Rams had the last shot.

Ben spread everybody out, kept his dribble, out near half-court, eyeballing the clock. Made his move with eight seconds to go, as soon as Shawn came up and set the high screen Sam used to set in moments like this.

Ben went around the screen, took it to the middle, into the lane.

Five seconds.

The defense collapsed on him, just the way he wanted, but when he looked over to the wing, where Sam always was, nobody was home. Shawn had stayed where he was after setting the screen, watching the action now instead of being a part of it.

Ben couldn't allow himself time to check the shot clock over the basket, knew he was up against the horn now, stepped back and let the ball go, shooting it higher than he normally would have wanted to get it over the long arms of Max Mahoney, the Parkerville center.

Another one that hit nothing but string.

Tie game.

Sam didn't even bother with his crutches, just got himself standing and hopped over to Ben, saying, "A fallaway? Seriously?"

"That's what happens when you lose your wingman," Ben said. "Sometimes you lose your mind."

After they'd all gotten their drinks, Coach gathered them around him underneath what was going to be their basket the second half, said, "Okay, now we've got to figure out a way to stop that guy."

"Which guy, Coach?" Coop said, trying to sound innocent.

Coach laughed. "The guy we're making look like his name should be Kobe LeBron Durant," he said. "We've run just about everybody we can at him, and nothing's worked. Not for lack of effort. Just because he's having one of those days, and one of those days can be the toughest thing to beat in sports sometimes. My feeling is we go back to the zone, make him keep making shots from the outside. If he does, we shake his hand at the end and say, 'Too tough.'"

Ben saw Coop raise a hand, his face full of fun.

"Coach," he said, "I think I speak for the whole team —"

"No," Sam said, "you don't."

As usual, Coop ignored him, kept going.

"We don't want to shake his hand and say, 'Too tough,' at the end," Coop said. "We mostly want to beat his —"

"I think we get your meaning," Coach said. "If the zone doesn't work, we'll have to go back to Plan B."

82

"Which is?" Ben said.

"The plan I haven't thought of yet," Coach Wright said.

The zone didn't work. Robbie stayed hot from the outside, got a couple of put-backs on the offensive boards, Parkerville stretched its lead back to twelve with a couple of minutes left in the third quarter, sat down again when he picked up his third foul.

Coach Wright had already done some subbing of his own, keeping everybody involved, the Rams made another little push with Robbie out of there, cut the lead down to six going into the fourth. It would be their starters against the Rockwell starters, maybe the whole rest of the way, depending on fouls, Robbie with his three, Shawn with three, Coop and MJ with four apiece.

In the huddle, Coach said, "Assistant Coach Brown has come up with Plan B."

He had their attention.

"We're playing a one-four defense the rest of the way," Coach said. "Our version of the old box-and-one."

He waited, knowing he *really* had their attention now, like he was telling a story and just now getting to the good parts, Ben feeling as if they were all leaning forward.

"Tell them what Plan B really means," Coach said to Sam.

And Sam said, "Plan B means Ben," looking right at Ben as he said, "The one on Robbie will be you, dude."

Ben said, "He's, like, twice my size."

"But only half as fast," Coach said. "Sam's right. Robbie can do a lot of things, but what he can't do is get around *you*. You pick him up as soon as he crosses halfcourt. If he brings it up, like he has sometimes, you pick him up in the *back-*court. Push him side to side as much as you can, and if he does get around you, we got the rest of the guys strung out like they're sitting on a fence."

"Coach, you know I'm up for this," Ben said. "But he can still shoot over me."

"Anytime he gets near one of his happy spots, we'll run Shawn at him or Darrelle or MJ. Or even Coop."

"You just annoy him as much as you possibly can," Sam said. "Pretend you're Coop."

"I'm standing right here!" Coop said.

They heard the whistle, broke the huddle. Sam said to Ben, "Go win the game."

The one-four bothered Robbie Burnett as much as Coach Wright — and Sam — hoped it would. Ben bothered him most of all.

Plan B McBain.

He felt like the point guard of the *defense* now. Not fixed on Chase Braggs today, or what had happened to Sam. Fixed on beating Parkerville.

Game tied again with four minutes left, Robbie's only points in the quarter on free throws. Ben went up for a jumper, saw Coop break open underneath, threw him a bullet pass, Coop made the layup.

Rams, 52–50. First lead of the game.

Robbie sold a great fake on a dribble-drive, stepped back, made a three.

Parkerville by a point now.

It was where they were when Coach Wright called a time-out, one minute and one second showing on the clock.

Sam grabbed Ben and said, "You know if it comes down to it, Robbie will try to do it all by himself."

"Yeah."

"If he does, overplay his right hand even more than you have been," Sam said. "I always did."

"Yeah, you did. You just did it much taller than I can."

"You got this," Sam said. "Make me look good."

"Trying, dude. Trying."

Last minute, close game. Ben thinking: Every game like this was different, every sport. But one thing never changed.

You got the chance to write the ending you wanted, every single time.

Rams ball, side out. Robbie walked past Sam, didn't make a big show of it, just put out a fist so Ben could tap it. Ben said in a quiet voice, "We gotta stop playing games like this."

And heard Robbie say, "Why?"

Forty-five seconds left now.

There was a thirty-five-second shot clock in their league, mostly so bad teams couldn't try to hold the ball all day against good teams. Ben just wanted to make sure that if the Rams got back up a point and the Patriots answered with a basket of their own, the Rams would still have the ball last and with enough time to set up a solid last shot.

Except.

Except Robbie had circled back and was guarding Ben now.

Parkerville had gone to their own Plan B.

Ben threw it in to Shawn who gave it right back to Ben. Now he was the one who couldn't get around Robbie. He couldn't worry about the clock now, or the last shot. Just the shot they needed to get the lead back.

He passed it to Shawn, Shawn passed it right back, ran behind the pass to set a screen. Now Ben was past Robbie, on the fly. A lot happened then. Coop's man came up to put himself between Ben and the basket. But Darrelle's guy scrambled in from the wing to cover Coop.

Ben kept his eyes locked on Coop, but he knew Darrelle had to be open, with the kind of space he needed. He was a good outside shooter, but he needed time to get his shot off. All the time in the world after Ben threw him a perfect, waist-high bounce pass.

Darrelle buried the jumper like a champion.

Rams back up a point.

Yeah, it was basketball season now, all right. All the season you could ever want. Thirty seconds left. The Patriots cleared out the right side for Robbie. And as much as Ben had bothered him down the stretch, as well as Sam's defense had looked, Robbie Burnett still looked as big as ever.

Ben was alone with him on the right side, watching Robbie eye's go to the clock over the basket. Ben gave a quick look to the shot clock at the other end.

Fifteen seconds now.

"Overplay," Sam had said.

Ben did.

But Robbie crossed over, crossed Ben up at the same time, going hard left for the first time the whole quarter.

Ten seconds.

Nine.

Robbie heading for the basket, Ben chasing, Coop coming up to give help, MJ scrambling to cover up on Coop's guy.

Six seconds.

But Ben knew Sam had been right, Robbie wasn't passing, he was going to try to make some kind of hero play, the kind he made an awful lot in football, win the game by himself.

Coop slid to his right just slightly, overplaying Robbie himself now, forcing him left. Again.

Ben looked up.

Three seconds.

Robbie Burnett stumbled slightly then, his right foot on top of Coop's, but knew he had to put something up, or lose the game, even if he was still dribbling with his left hand.

Everything about the shot looked wrong, Robbie shooting it off his wrong foot, almost from his hip, Coop nearly getting a hand on it.

Everything looked wrong until Ben saw the ball come off Robbie's left hand with perfect rotation on it, saw the ball hit the middle of the square above the basket almost dead center, saw the ball fall through the rim as if Robbie had called "backboard" in a game of H-O-R-S-E.

Ben had made the right play. They all had.

Whole game came out wrong, for the Rams, anyway.

By a point.

Ben's dad had told him a story one time, when they were watching the Packers play in a near blizzard, about this famous field goal some old Giants kicker had made one time. It was a long one, but because the snow that day was totally covering the yardage lines by the end of that game, no one was sure how far it was.

Still: When the kicker came off the field, one of his coaches said, "You know you can't kick it that far."

Ben felt that way about Robbie Burnett's shot: The guy had to know there was no way he could have made a shot like that to win a game.

But then again, Robbie felt that way after Ben threw the pass to Sam to win the football championship.

Maybe that was why, right after the ball went through the basket, Robbie turned around to find Ben. And smiled. And Ben smiled back.

Robbie came walking over to him, shaking his head, and the two of them did one of those lean-in, half hugs.

Ben spoke first.

"A lefty bank shot? Really?"

Robbie said, "That Hail Mary to Sam? Really?"

Sometimes in sports you ended up on the exact same page, even if only one of you got the ending he wanted.

There was a lot going on around them. But it was just Robbie and Ben at the top of the key. Robbie's teammates knowing enough to give them room, give them a minute.

"That was an awesome game of basketball, no lie," Ben said.

"Back at you."

"Maybe we'll see you guys in another championship game," Ben said, even if that was such a mad crazy idea right now, the Rams being 0–2 and Ben sure that somewhere Chase Braggs and Darby were going to 2–0.

"Fine by me," Robbie said and then he went to celebrate with his guys, because that is what you did after you won a game the way the Parkerville Patriots just had.

Sam was coming for Ben now, Ben not surprised at how well Sam could move on his crutches, like learning to get around on them was just one more thing he was going to make look easy, the way he did with sports.

"I was the one who had the brilliant idea to force him left," Sam said.

"I made the right play," Ben said. "Coop made the right play. Robbie just made a better one." Ben lifted his shoulders, let them drop, said, "Great players make great plays. You do it all the time."

"So do you."

"Came up one play short today."

Sam shook his head now. "Lefty. He looked like he was *bowling* the ball at the hoop."

"Nearly fell on his face."

"Coop hanging all over him and somehow not fouling him."

"Like John McEnroe says," Ben said. "You *cannot* be serious."

Coach Wright was waving the Rams over to the bench now, telling them there wasn't much to say, other than this: That they'd play a great game, shouldn't hang their heads, should be proud of the way they came back, they just got beat, it happened in sports.

"Don't let a loss like this crush you," Coach said. "That's an order." And went across the court to talk to the Parkerville coach, Mr. Crockett.

Ben didn't need Coach to tell him. He didn't feel crushed. Disappointed, yeah. Still shocked the ball had gone in. Knowing that with an 0–2 record things just got harder in a league that had Chase and Robbie and where they didn't have Sam.

Mostly he felt proud of his team today, is what he felt, sitting where he'd sat listening to Coach. They'd given all they had and it wasn't enough.

"What?" Sam said.

"I didn't say anything."

"Maybe not to me," Sam said. "But I can always tell when there's a lot of talking going on inside your head."

"You want to know what I was really just thinking?" Ben said. "How cool it was to play that game."

"But we lost. And I know you're the worst loser in the world, even if you don't always show it to the rest of the world."

"*I* know," Ben said.

Looked over at Sam and said, "Weird, huh?"

Totally.

Ben not knowing at the time that things were about to get even more weird before the day was over.


"You want me to do *what*?" Ben said to Lily.

The two of them out on the old swings, out near the basketball court at McBain Field, Lily having been waiting for Ben when he got home from the game, having had a sleepover at her friend Molly's house the night before.

"I want you to go to the movies tomorrow," she said, "even though you're acting as if I asked you to clean your room."

"You're not just asking me to go to a movie," he said. "You're asking me to go to a movie with Chase Braggs. And I would rather clean my room, and yours, than do *that*."

"You're just being silly," Lily said. "And it's not you just going to a movie with Chase. You're going with me, and Molly, and Jeb. And Chase."

Jeb Arcelus. Molly's brother. Chase's teammate on the Darby team. Molly being the one who'd first given Lily the intel on the new hoops hotshot in Darby.

"And, by the way," Lily said, "I thought *we* had agreed that *you* were no longer going to treat Chase like some sort of swamp thingy."

Somehow Lily had known as much about the game as if she'd watched it herself. Ben wasn't surprised. Hardly anything about Lily Wyatt surprised him. He would actually have been surprised if she *didn't* have all the important intel of the day.

But they had stopped swinging as soon as Lily had told him about her big movie plan for tomorrow afternoon, a new vampire movie having just opened at the Palace Theater on Main Street.

The plan that included Chase Braggs.

"You know I've chilled on that guy," Ben said. "But that doesn't mean I want to hang out with him. And I don't even like vampire movies."

"You'll be hanging around with *me*," Lily said. "And other people will get to feel cool hanging around with *us*."

Yeah, Ben thought, *really* cool.

"Sounds like you've already been hanging around with him," Ben said.

Lily recoiled, like she'd seen a snake appear in the dirt in front of them. "Oooh," she said, "*him*. Swamp Thing."

"Go ahead," Ben said, "have your little fun. But you *were* hanging out with him. And shouldn't he have had a game today?"

"Something about their gym, they had to play in the morning," Lily said. "When the game was over, Jeb and Chase came back to their house, is all. I wouldn't call it hanging out."

"I would."

"Molly was the one who actually came up with the movie plan," Lily said.

"Oh, so you're throwing her under the bus."

"For making a plan to go to a *movie*?"

"And Chase Braggs was cool with going to that movie with *me*?"

"I didn't say he was cool," Lily said, "just that he'd feel cool hanging with us."

"You didn't answer my question."

Lily smiled. "He was fine with it."

"Are you gonna ask Sam and Shawn and Coop to come, too?"

Lily said, "I just wanted to run it by the leader of the pack first. Who I know, in his heart of hearts, wants to go to the movies tomorrow with me."

Then she pushed back and pushed off and was swinging again, hair flying, looking happy.

Being Lily.

Ben stayed where he was. Knowing — in his heart of hearts — he was in a bad spot. He didn't want to hang with Chase Braggs in ten million years, that was for sure. And he wanted to hang out with Chase *and* Lily even less, whether there'd be other guys along for the ride or not.

On her way by, Lily said, "Well?"

She had him and she knew it.

Stopped swinging again.

"Do I ever say no to you?"

"Um, *that* would be a no from me."

"Because I know and you know that if I said I didn't want to go you'd call me a wimp," he said. "Or a big baby."

"Big Ben McBain?" It was something only she called him. "A big baby? Never."

"Yeah, right."

"C'mon, it'll be fun."

"Fine. I'll do it," he said.

She made a motion like she was pulling a chain toward her and said, *"Yes!"* Completely happy with herself, having gotten what she wanted, which she usually did.

Another part of being Lily.

"And you're saying yes because you know I'm right, and it will be fun," she said.

She was wrong.

Ben was only saying yes because he really did know there was no way in the world he could say no.

Because no way in this world he was going to let Chase Braggs go to a movie with Lily without him.

Ever since he'd tried to make his attitude adjustment about Chase, he'd only been thinking about basketball, that it really wasn't just him against Chase, that basketball *was* a five-man game, that it was never just one-on-one.

So why did a trip to the movies on a Sunday afternoon feel exactly like that now?

Like he was competing with Chase all over again?

# 14

At first Sam and Coop and Shawn said forget it, no way they were going to the movies with a guy from another team, especially *that* guy, they'd rather have some teeth pulled than hang out with Chase Braggs.

They were all in Ben's basement, having finished playing video games for the moment, switching back and forth between college basketball games. It was a sleepover Saturday night, this time at Ben's, two guys sleeping on couches, two on blow-up mattresses.

Shawn was the first to change his mind, saying that he'd provide Ben with backup.

"That's it, I'm in," Shawn said.

"Get out," Coop said. "You don't want to go any more than we do."

"But Ben would do the same for any one of us," Shawn said.

"And I already told Lily I would go," Ben said.

"I get that," Coop said. "What I don't get is why."

There was a chair in front of Sam, a couple of pillows on it,

Sam's ankle propped up on the pillows. He looked at Coop and said, "How dense are you?"

Coop grinned. "On a good day or a bad one?"

Sam said, "He's going because he's *not* gonna let Chase go to the movies with Lily alone."

"She won't be alone with him," Ben said.

"In your brain she will," Sam said.

"And you still won't go with me?"

"Too much weirdness, too little fun," Sam said. "And I don't like dopey vampire movies any more than you do."

Shawn said, "Wouldn't us not going be a violation of the Cooper Manley Bro Code?"

Lots of guys had some kind of bro code. Coop's Bro Code — for the Core Four plus Shawn — just seemed to be the one with the most rules to it, Coop constantly revising it, depending on the situation.

"Shawn's right!" Ben said. "Hadn't even thought of that. *Definite* violation of the Bro Code."

He looked at Coop now, who had slumped back in his chair, frowning, deep in thought. Or as deep as he ever got.

"Right, Coop?" Ben said.

Coop held up a finger now, like a great idea had just come to him, and said, "The Bro Code does not apply to a total *non*-bro like Chase Braggs-A-Lot."

Coop turned to Sam and said, "Help a brother out here. Or bro."

"I would," Sam said, "except for the fact that you're pretty much beyond help."

"Why don't you all just help *me*?" Ben said.

Coop said, "What I really don't get is that you're actually going to miss a Packers game to go to a movie with the hated Chase?"

"I don't hate him," Ben said. "I just want to beat him."

"Do you want to beat him in a game," Sam said, grinning, "or give him a beat*down* because he likes Lily?"

"Who said he likes Lily?" Ben said.

"Or," Sam said, "is this all because you think Lily might actually like *him*?"

Ben knew Sam was right. And that Sam probably knew that Ben knew he was right. So there was no reason for Ben to pretend that he wasn't. Or that it wasn't true. Because it was.

That was exactly what he was worried about.

Now Sam said, "Okay, I'm in, too."

"Same," Coop said.

He shifted position with his ankle a little bit, Ben seeing him make a face as he did, and said, "Plus, this might be the first time in history that there's a better show in the seats than there is on the screen."

"The more I think about it," Coop said, "the more I can't wait till tomorrow."

Ben sighing again, thinking:

Tomorrow's a long day already.

# 15

Chase didn't try to sit next to Lily once they were inside the theater, staying at the other end of the row with Jeb and Molly Arcelus.

But now he was right next to Lily at the big round table in the back room at Pinocchio's Pizza, getting to the seat before Ben could do anything about it. Like he'd spotted an opening on the basketball court and didn't hesitate making his move.

Yeah, Ben said to himself.

Making his move.

So he was over there, Lily to his right and Jeb to his left. Molly Arcelus was on Lily's right, Coop next to *her* and looking pretty happy to be there.

Ben, Sam, and Shawn were across from them.

Chase and Ben hadn't said very much to each other when they'd all met in front of the theater, and then nothing once they were inside.

But now Chase said, "Heard you guys lost a tough one yesterday."

Trying to sound as if he cared. Maybe for Lily's benefit.

"It was a great game," Ben said. Trying not to act steamed that Chase was sitting where he was as he said, "Guy made a crazy shot at the end."

"Robbie Burnett," Chase said.

Ben said, "You ever see him play?"

"Heard about him," Chase said. "All the guys on our team who played against him in football say he's the best guy in our league in two sports. They say he's totally off the hook as a quarterback."

Ben was going to let that one go. Sam didn't. His chair against the wall next to where he had his crutches. Wounded, but still a wingman.

"Don't know how that's possible," Sam said, "since everybody knows he isn't even the best QB in our league because Ben is."

Sam hadn't managed to knock the smile off Chase's face. Before he could say anything, Ben said, "And I don't see how he could be the best two-sport guy because Sam is."

"When he's not stepping in holes playing one-on-one with you, right?" Chase said.

Still smiling. Looking at Ben as he said it.

Both of them knowing that the air around the table had changed now. Ben's eyes shifted just enough to see Lily looking at Chase, then Ben, Lily knowing that there was definitely some chirp going on at Pinocchio's. The only time Lily Wyatt missed anything was when she was sleeping, and Ben wasn't sure she missed much then.

She clapped her hands now, the sound loud, looking like a

teacher decided to call a class to order, and said, "How about we order up some pies?"

But as soon as they did, Chase said, "It must be weird for you guys after the way football ended, starting out hoops 0–2."

Shawn said, "We started out 0–2 in football. Long season, dude."

Chase looked at Shawn as if noticing him for the first time. "Lily said you started out the season as the quarterback, right?"

Shawn nodded, said, "I was only the starter until we figured out who the best QB was."

"And that the best tight end was you," Ben said.

They bumped fists on that one.

"Still, that must have been weird," Chase said to Shawn. "Your dad being the coach and all."

Now Coop jumped in, saying to Chase, "What have you been doing, taking a course in Rockwell sports since you moved to Darby?"

"Lily just filled me in on you guys, is all," Chase said.

"Well, only because you *asked*," Lily said.

"Just trying to learn as much as I can about the competition," Chase said.

Ben wasn't sure if he meant in basketball, or some competition for Lily's friendship.

"Nothing wrong with that, right, Lily?" Chase said, turning to her.

"Don't try to drag me into one of these guys' dramas," Lily said. "Girls get called drama queens, but I've always sort of thought it was boys who were kings."

Chase wasn't going to let it go.

"What drama?" he said. "You were the one who told me that things *were* pretty awkward for a while between Ben and Shawn."

"Only until Shawn and I got to know each other," Ben said.

"Yeah," Coop said, leaning forward, all the way into *this* conversation now. "Funny how that works out sometimes. Sometimes the more you get to know somebody the more you like them." Now he smiled at Chase and said, "And sometimes you like them less."

The drinks were delivered to the table then and the two large pizzas were right behind them, Ben hoping that the food and drinks would change the subject. Whatever the subject really was.

But all through lunch, he had to watch Chase talking quietly to Lily, like the rest of them had finished lunch and left, Chase seeming to laugh at every other thing Lily said. Giving a quick look over at Ben every couple of minutes, as if trying to make sure that Ben was watching.

But Ben knew that as much as Chase had gone out of his way to annoy him, the day was almost over, that he was going to have survived a whole afternoon with the guy without telling him what an idiot he thought he was.

Or acting like an idiot himself.

Wrong.

While they were all getting their money out, Chase said to Ben, "Must crush you, having given up the game-winner in the first two games of the season, right?"

Ben smiled a smile he wasn't feeling, shrugged, and said, "Not much to say." Then went back to counting all the dollar bills everybody had tossed to the middle of the table like that was the most important job he was going to have all weekend. Or maybe ever.

Like he was trying to run out the clock.

"Funny thing about McBain," Sam said. "He never says much. Win *or* lose."

Chase put on what Ben hoped was the last fake smile he'd have to look at until the next time they played.

"Yeah, Ben's the best, no doubt," Chase said. "That's what everybody says. Best QB. Best teammates. Best friend. Hey, even best boyfriend."

Lily looked as if she was about to say something, but didn't.

Ben said, "Stop."

"Stop what?" Chase said, trying to sound innocent.

"Stop busting my bones," Ben said. "About Robbie, about losing our first two games, about Sam's ankle. About everything."

"Take a chill pill, dude," Chase said. "You're, like, way too sensitive."

"No," Ben said, "I'm not."

Just him and Chase now, like at the end of another game. Everybody watching them, nobody else saying anything, maybe because they didn't know what to say.

Ben stood up, reached over and got Sam's crutches from him, helped Sam out of his chair.

Shawn and Coop were up, too.

Lily was still sitting there, as if she didn't know what her next move should be, since this had been her idea. This was her party.

Then it just came out, Ben saying to her, "I can't believe you wanted me to hang out with this guy. I can't believe *you* want to hang out with this guy."

And now it had happened just the way Sam had joked that it would, even though this was no joke. Ben *had* become a better show than the movie, not able to stop himself before the clock did run out on this whole stupid afternoon, not knowing what else to do now except turn and walk out with Sam and Coop and Shawn.

He walked into the front room at Pinocchio's and past the counter, not looking back, feeling like he'd lost to Chase Braggs again.

Ben tried calling Lily when he got home, got her machine, decided not to leave a message.

He knew what he had to do and wanted to do it as soon as possible: Apologize for saying what he'd said about her and Chase, for walking out the way he did without even saying good-bye. He knew that Chase had gotten exactly what he wanted, for Ben to look like the jerk even though it was Chase who had been acting like one from the time he made sure he sat next to Lily at Pinocchio's.

But Ben knew it wasn't the little comments Chase kept making that got him mad, he knew better than that because he knew him*self* better than that:

It was seeing Chase with Lily on the other side of the table.

The two of them laughing it up the way they were, like all of a sudden there was a new club that only included the two of them. Ben knew it was more Chase than Lily, obviously. Lily wasn't really *doing* anything. Or encouraging Chase. Chase had just taken over, doing most of the talking, telling stories about his old hometown, about new teachers and his new teammates, the differences between the way kids he'd grown up with talked in the Midwest and the way they talked here, saying he worried that he wasn't cool enough to live in the east. Yeah, right, Ben thought, listening — and listening — to Chase be the big talker here the way he was on a basketball court. Lily was mostly listening, too.

And doing a whole lot of laughing.

But as far as Ben could tell, it wasn't like she was being made to do any of it against her will.

*That* bothered Ben a whole lot more than the way he'd acted on his way out the door.

When they'd gotten outside, waiting for Shawn's mom to come pick them up — Ben hoping that she showed up before Lily and the Darby kids came through the door — Coop had said, "I thought that went well."

Being Coop, trying to joke away the tension they were all feeling or at least joke it down.

"Not now, Coop," Sam said.

Coop put up both hands and said, "Shutting up now."

Nobody said another word until they were inside Mrs. O'Brien's big SUV.

Now Ben was alone in his room, not ready to go downstairs and watch the second game of the NFL doubleheader with his dad.

Out loud he said, "Things are going *awesome* these days."

He went through the list, one by one. Sam was hurt. Team was 0–2. Chase Braggs wasn't just getting the better of him in basketball now, he showed he could do it just going for pizza. Lily was probably mad at Ben, really mad, something that hardly ever happened.

And on top of all that? Ben was sure that somewhere Chase was smiling his stupid head off, feeling like he'd won something on a day when he hadn't even played a game.

Yeah. *Totally* awesome stretch Ben was having. The way things had turned out today, losing to Robbie Burnett and Parkerville yesterday was starting to look like the highlight of his weekend.

Ben stared out the window for a while, last of the afternoon light, decided that there was still enough light to go shoot around at McBain. Grabbed his basketball, went down the stairs, out the door, pounding the ball hard as soon as he hit the sidewalk, pounding it even harder once he got out on the road.

A funny thing happened then.

Not funny like Mr. Funny, Chase Braggs.

Funny in a different way.

Ben got mad. Not just about today, not just about Chase.

He got mad at himself, for the way he was starting to turn into Poor-Me McBain, the way he was feeling so sorry for himself. Like he really was the one who had gotten hurt.

He got to the court and pulled up and put up a shot from three-point distance, made it, nothing but net.

Enough, Ben told himself.

*Enough.*

Enough bad stuff had happened, on and off the court.

Time to change that.

He ran over, collected the ball, ran back outside, put up another shot.

Buried that one.

Ben was sure it probably didn't look to anybody else at Rockwell Middle School — or the rest of the Core Four plus Shawn — as if anything had changed between Ben and Lily.

But it had, at least for now.

Ben knew Lily well enough, knew how true-blue she was, to know that what had happened at Pinocchio's wasn't going to mess them up forever.

Just for now.

When they walked home from school together on Monday, Ben apologized for the way he'd acted. Lily had said, "Apology accepted. Now shut up." And he had.

They still talked on the computer at night. Had lunch together in the cafeteria almost every day. Walked to classes together. Everything looking the same.

Just different.

Like there was more they needed to be talking about. *Stuff.* The kind of stuff girls loved to talk about and guys hated. And when there was stuff that Lily thought she needed to talk out with Ben, she was the one who always brought it up, not him.

Sometimes it wasn't anything bad going on between them, sometimes Lily liked to talk about the fact that boys didn't.

Like to talk.

One day on the swings, way before Chase came into the picture, she'd said, "You know what the real Bro Code is for bros?"

"Please educate me."

"The real Bro Code is only talking about whatever's bothering you bros as a last resort. And you know who's worse than anybody? *You!*"

And Ben had said that day, "Maybe I'm *better* at it, that would be a more positive way of looking at things."

And Lily had sighed and said, *"Guys."*

So after he apologized, he went back to being a guy, not asking what was really bothering her even though he knew something was.

Not because he didn't think it was any of his business, because up until now he considered everything happening in Lily's life to be part of his business.

No, it wasn't that.

Ben knew the real reason he wasn't asking the question is because he didn't want to know the answer, at least for now. For now he wanted to focus all of his energy — good and bad — on the Rams' next game, on the road, against the Kingsland Knights. Ben still didn't know how the season was going to play out without Sam, if they could be anything more than some mediocre .500 team. Or worse. Even though he'd thrown himself into practice like a madman all week, there was a part of Ben worrying about playing as well as they all had against Robbie Burnett's team and still losing.

He just wasn't going to tell his teammates that. He was going to Kingsland and he was coming back with the win that meant they didn't start the season 0–3. His whole life his dad had found different ways of telling him the same story over and over again, about how you had to get back up after getting knocked down, in sports or anything else.

Time to get up against Kingsland.

The Knights had become one of Ben's favorite basketball opponents last season because their best player, Jamal Warren, was a point guard, too.

He was small the way Ben was, and fast, and smart, and good with the ball and fun and all of that made him fun to play against, Ben almost feeling as if he were going up against himself.

Jamal Warren played the game with a smile the way Chase Braggs did, just not a phony smile, or a cocky one. Jamal was never woofing on you when he smiled at you on a basketball court, or acting like he thought he was better than you, or wanting to show you up. *His* smile was all about the ball he was playing against you, all about competing.

After Ben and Jamal high-fived each other at halfcourt right before the game was supposed to start, Jamal said, "Heard about Sam, yo. Bad break."

Jamal was just about the only kid Ben knew who could carry off "yo" and not sound silly doing it.

"About the only good part," Ben said, "was that the bad break wasn't in his ankle."

"Still not counting you out today," Jamal said.

"That would be a mistake," Ben said, then grinning and adding, "Yo."

"Hope you have more game playing against me than you do trying to talk like me," Jamal said, and then bumped him some fist and went to be with his team and Ben did the same.

The game against Jamal and the Knights started out, first half, like the game the Rams had played the week before against Parkerville. They fell behind early because the other team's star player — Jamal — came out hot. Then caught up before the second quarter was over because Shawn and Darrelle started making everything they looked at.

Rams 28, Knights 28, at the half.

Ben and Jamal had gotten after each other the way they had last season, Jamal with more points so far, Ben with more assists. Ben had gotten one steal off Jamal, Jamal had done the same to him. The only problem with Jamal's steal was that Ben had made it worse by catching up with him, fouling him more out of dumb frustration than anything else when he should have just let him make the layup that would have tied the game with two seconds left in the half.

Ben's third foul of the game.

Bonehead move, especially for somebody who prided himself on being a smart player. Jamal made the free throw, Ben fired up a shot at the buzzer from halfcourt that fell way short, game tied. Bad ending, good half, and Ben knew it. He was even smiling as he walked over to Sam and said, "Scale of one to ten, how dumb was that foul?"

112

"Ten," Sam said, smiling back. "Seriously? You were just trying way too hard to make up for a dumb mistake, is all. And you've played with three fouls plenty of times and never fouled out."

Ben knew Sam was right. He was steamed right now about the foul, but steamed in a good way, remembering the promise he'd made — to himself — about having a good attitude no matter what, even when things weren't going his way.

"I'm just down with winning this game," he said.

"And we're gonna win," Sam said. "You're playing your butt off, you've got everybody involved today. For real. Just do us all a huge favor and don't commit your fourth foul anytime soon."

"How about never?" Ben said.

"Even better," Sam said.

Ben couldn't pick up his fourth at the start of the third quarter because Coach sat him, not putting him back out there until there were two minutes left, the Knights up six by then. Ben immediately threw a perfect pass to Shawn on the wing, but Shawn missed, the Knights got a long rebound, suddenly it was Jamal and their shooting guard on a two-on-one.

Ben was the one.

Jamal passed the ball at the top of the key, but Ben was sure it was coming back to him. When it did, he had perfect position on him, Jamal already up in the air, Ben getting his feet set and his body squared up.

Taking the charge as Jamal put a knee in his chest and they both went down hard, Ben looking up to see that somehow the shot Jamal had thrown up had gone in, the ref blowing his whistle on the offensive foul.

Only he didn't call it that way, he put both hands on his hips and called a block on Ben.

Ben, who never questioned a ref's call, ever, jumped to his feet and said, "I wasn't moving!"

"Son," the ref said. "I make the calls. You play. That's the way it works."

"But, ref . . ." Ben said.

The ref came over, smiling at Ben, quietly saying, "Son, butt *out*."

His fourth foul, before the fourth quarter had even begun. Coach took him out. Sam made room for him, moving one seat over. Ben sat down hard and said, "My feet were *set*."

"I know," Sam said.

"Me, too," Coach Wright said.

"Coach, I can play the fourth quarter with four fouls," Ben said.

Coach patted him on the shoulder and said, "Know that, too."

By the time the quarter ended, though, the Rams were down ten. Staring at a potential 0–3 start the way Ben kept staring at the scoreboard.

He didn't have to ask to go back out for the fourth quarter, even with those four fouls. Coach just turned to him and said, "You're gonna be there at the start of the quarter, and still out there at the end of the game. Got it?" Ben nodded, then listened as Coach Wright said, "Here's all my wisdom for the rest of this game: Go win it."

They put their hands together, broke the huddle. As they did, Sam whacked him with one of his crutches and said, "Jamal's tired."

"Right," Ben said. "He gets tired about as often as I get tired."

"I'm telling you, the guy's dragging," Sam said. "He's got no push when he shoots from the outside, it's why he missed his last couple of shots. Start picking him up fullcourt."

"How come you never did this much coaching before you got hurt?"

Sam said, "Didn't have to. Had you."

But he was right. Jamal *was* starting to act a little gassed, and Ben making him work bringing the ball up the court didn't even allow him to have a quick breather doing *that*.

And for the first time the whole game, Jamal wasn't smiling.

With four minutes left, Ben stole the ball from Jamal at the top of the key, started a fast break, fed Coop for his first basket of the game. Knights 40, Rams 34. Ben still had those four fouls. They were still looking at 0–3 if they couldn't win the last four minutes. But Ben felt the game changing.

Felt like something good was finally about to happen in the basketball season.

Jamal may have been tired, but wasn't done, came down and made a crazy off-balance three from the corner, falling out of bounds as the ball went through the basket. Knights back up nine. Coach Wright jumped up and called time, waved them over, telling them to hurry, like he couldn't wait to give the pep talk Ben knew he was about to give them.

They all took seats, he knelt down in front of them, said, "Plenty of time. Pretty simple plan, too: Get a score, get a stop. Then do that again."

Coop grinned. "*Now* you tell us."

Coach looked up at all of them and said, "Boys, the next few minutes are gonna turn our whole season around."

This was one more time, Ben knew, when Coach Keith Wright was trying to make his belief theirs.

Ben came down the right side, left-hand dribbled toward the free throw line, wheeled, and threw it to Shawn on the right wing. Where Sam always was. Shawn didn't hesitate, even though he hadn't made a shot for a while, knocked down the three.

Just like that they were down six again, 43–37.

Still down six with just under two minutes left. Jamal ran some clock, like he'd been doing, got a step on Ben. This time it was Coop stepping between Jamal and the hoop, Coop trying to draw the foul. Coop didn't flop, he hated guys who flopped trying to draw fouls, just stood there and took the hit.

This time the Rams got the whistle, the ref putting his hand to the back of his head, meaning offensive foul. Coop nodded, turned to Ben, pointed. Ben took the inbounds pass from him, pushed the ball hard up the court, got inside, wanting to kick it to either Darrelle on the left wing or Shawn on the right. Both smothered. Ben didn't hesitate, put up a *sweet* teardrop over Jamal Warren, money all the way.

Down four.

"Score and stop," Coach had said.

They got the stop, Darrell made a wide-open jumper off a feed from Ben at the other end. Down two. The Knights' shooting guard made a wide-open jumper of his own. Rams still down four. Ben went back to Darrelle. Outside the three-point line this time. Darrelle held his shooting pose, sure that he'd made it. He had.

Now the Rams were down one.

Thirty-eight seconds left.

Lot of ways this could go. The Knights could just hold it for thirty-five seconds, dare the Rams to get off a good shot with the three seconds they had left. Or the Rams could foul.

Or the Rams could get one more stop.

Ben didn't even wait to hear from Coach, yelled, "No fouls!" at his teammates. Doing what point guards are supposed to do, being the coach on the floor that the coach of the team expected him to be.

Jamal stood and dribbled the ball near the midcourt line, eyes shifting from Ben to the shot clock over the basket. Ben checking the shot clock over the Rams' basket, opposite end. Ben more sure than ever that Jamal was going to drive the ball to the basket, either score or draw a foul. Or both.

Twelve seconds left.

"Go!" Jamal's coach yelled.

It was just enough to distract him, Jamal turning his head just slightly, Ben going for the ball as he did, getting a hand on it, swiping it toward the sideline.

He and Jamal seemed to have the same shot at the ball, until they didn't, Ben hearing Coach Wright's voice inside his head, that voice yelling at him the way he always yelled at practice when they'd have loose-ball drills:

"Who wants it more?"

I do.

Ben got to the ball a stride before it went out of bounds, knowing it would be off him if it did go out, not knowing the time, just knowing there couldn't be much of it left in Kingsland.

Got his right hand on the ball. As he did, saw a streak of blue — the Rams were in their blue road uniforms — heading toward their basket.

Ben didn't hesitate, just wheeled and threw the ball as hard as he could in that direction, saw at the same time who it was.

MJ.

MJ: Who hadn't even taken a shot yet in a real game, who'd bricked the two free throws he'd attempted in the Parkerville game the week before.

MJ caught up with the ball at the top of the key, Ben seeing there were three seconds left now at the same time MJ did. MJ deciding in that moment there wasn't enough time for him to drive in for a layup.

Ben could only watch helplessly from where he was standing, watch the way everybody else in Kingsland's gym did, watch as MJ pushed off on the wrong foot, looking as if he were somehow falling down a flight of stairs as he pushed his shot toward the basket, releasing the ball right before the clock showed one second left.

Ben: Watching in disbelief as MJ's shot, so high it looked like it might bounce off the shot clock, kissed the very top of the backboard and dropped through the net as the Rams went from losing another game to finally winning one.

More than anything, Ben was happiest for MJ Lau.

The guy who hadn't made the team two years in a row. The guy who needed Sam getting hurt to get his spot this year. The guy who hadn't scored and really *couldn't* score hitting the game-winning basket.

Looking as happy now on the court as sports could ever possibly make you.

First he ran straight for Ben, Ben afraid in that moment that MJ was going to plow right through him the way he did to opposing players when they got in his way. Like he might get whistled for one more foul even though the game was over and the Rams had won.

He stopped just short and chest-bumped Ben instead, Ben happy he'd braced himself for whatever was about to happen, because it would have been a little embarrassing having a teammate's chest bump put him down.

"Thank you!" MJ said.

"You're welcome," Ben said. "But for what, exactly?"

"Passing me the ball!"

"Dude, you were open."

"Are you *insane*?" MJ said. "I'm open all the time and guys don't throw me the ball."

"Well this time I did," Ben said. "And you made the shot. And if you can make *that* shot with the game on the line, you know what that means, right?"

"Help me out."

"It means you're a scorer now."

"I am?" MJ said. Like it was still a question for him. But then he smiled and nodded his head and said, "I *am*!"

MJ ran up into the stands then, up to where his dad was, MJ's dad waiting for him the way Ben's always did, waiting for a hug.

When Ben turned back around, Jamal was standing there, hand stretched straight out for Ben to shake.

"You got me this time," he said.

"Got lucky, is all."

"Nah," Jamal, smiling again, said. "Was no luck involved. You read me perfectly. Forgot at the worst possible time I can't let up for one second going against a guy like you."

"Good playing against you," Ben said.

Meaning it.

"Same."

"Maybe we'll see you in the playoffs," Ben said, but Jamal said, "Nah, we're not good enough."

Maybe we aren't, either, Ben thought after Jamal walked away. Maybe we're just not this season, not without Sam. But as Ben walked toward Sam now, Ben feeling a smile of his own coming over him, he thought this, too:

We were good enough today.

*Just.*

Sam said, "So this is what winning feels like, huh?"

"Almost forgot."

"It *has* only been a few weeks since football."

"Dude, a lot has happened since," Ben said. "*Too* much."

"Let's just enjoy this one at least until we get home," Sam said. "You're the one always telling me the biggest game is the one we're playing."

"Or just played."

"Yeah," Sam said. "That, too."

"If we can win one like this," Ben said, "maybe miracles can still happen for us."

They both turned at the same time, saw MJ still up in the stands, high-fiving other kids' parents now.

"One just did," Sam said.

Ben and Sam went back and sat down in front of Coach Wright with the rest of the guys, as Coach said, "Boys, that one was just pure good."

And that's the way Ben was feeling right now, first time in a while, hoping the feeling would last.

Pure good.

Not bad.


Usually when he'd get home after a game like this, a win like this, Lily would be waiting for him.

Lily would know about the game, because she always knew. Win or lose. She might wait a little longer sometimes if it was a loss, just to give Ben some room. But if it was a really bad loss, she'd be right there, sitting on his front porch or waiting inside with Ben's parents if somebody else had given him a ride home.

Lily: Who'd tell him it was just a silly old game if the Rams had lost or making it sound like practically the greatest win in the whole world if they'd won.

Just not today.

She wasn't waiting for him at the house when Mr. O'Brien dropped off him and Sam and Coop and Shawn. When Ben tried to call her house, he got the answering machine. No e-mails from her on his laptop when he ran up to his room to check, telling the guys he'd be right back, he wanted to grab his Packers sweatshirt in case they went outside.

No message on the McBains' phone.

No text message on the cell phone he'd only had for a month.

No Lily.

So things still weren't normal between them, even though she'd accepted his apology — Monday, at school — for the way he'd acted at Pinocchio's.

If things were normal, he knew, he would have heard from her by now. She would have texted him about the game. Or come over. Or called. But she hadn't. Her call, Ben thought. It had been too great a day, too great a finish, too great a win for him to let a girl ruin it. Even the best girl Ben knew.

He threw on his sweatshirt, walked down the stairs, already hearing the laughter from the basement.

Ben went down there to be with his boys.

Saturday before Christmas. Second regular-season game against Darby. Darby's gym.

Rams at 2–2, having beaten Glendale at Glendale the previous Saturday. The Bears still undefeated, a perfect 4–0.

Rockwell vs. Darby, again. Ben vs. Chase, even if Ben had been telling himself all week that the object of the game wasn't for him to beat Chase Braggs on Chase's home court. It was to get the Rams over .500.

If they could beat the Bears, they'd go into the break with a 3–2 record and the Bears would be 4–1. One game separating them in the standings. Game on.

Two wins in a row now for the Rams. So things were getting better in basketball for Ben. And with Lily, ever since his apology, still not great, like there was something between them, something they still weren't talking about.

But a little better.

Ben was trying to explain it to Sam on the way to Darby, Ben's mom driving her new SUV, Ben and Sam and Coop in the backseat, Shawn in the way-backseat.

"It sounds, dear," Ben's mom said, "as if this Chase is still the elephant in the room." And then explained to them that the elephant in the room meant something nobody wanted to talk about.

"More like the donkey in the room, if you ask me," Coop said.

"Good one, Coop," Sam said.

Coop blew out some air and said, "Wow, I don't hear that one very much."

Shawn said, "Is Lily coming today?"

Ben said, "She said she was."

"To an away game?" Coop said.

"Uh, I think she slept over at Molly's last night," Ben said.

"So she was in Darby last night?" Sam said. "You think that brought the Chase factor into play?"

Ben said, "Why don't you ask her?" knowing he sounded way too chafed, not able to do anything about it.

"C'mon, I'm just playin'," Sam said.

"Time to talk about playing this *game*," Ben said, and so that's what they did for the rest of the ride to Darby Middle School, telling one another that today's game was going to be different from the others against Chase Braggs and the Darby Bears.

And it was.

Lily *was* there, Ben saw her a few minutes before the game started, sitting up behind the Rams' bench, smiling at Ben and waving when she caught his eye.

Mouthing: *Good luck.*

Ben waved back and then, because he could feel Lily's eyes still on him, ran over to shake hands with Chase Braggs.

"Have a good one," he said.

"Hey," Chase said, "they've all been good ones for us so far."

Ben started to pull away, but Chase still had a grip on his right hand. The two of them at halfcourt, all the other players from both teams shooting around.

"Well," Ben said, trying to pull back, "let's get after it."

Chase finally released his hand, saying, "Gotta look good in front of Lily, right?"

"Right," Ben said, and ran down to be with his teammates, wondering which one of them would look better today.

He did early. Ben did and the Rams did. Both the first and second units. Offense and defense. Acting as if the Bears' house was their house. Playing as if they were the best team in the Butler County League, as if they were the ones who were undefeated.

Coach started the game with Ben guarding Chase, but after that kept switching up his defenses: man, zone, box-and-one, fullcourt press, sometimes trap press. When they went back to man, it would be Darrelle on Chase, or Shawn, even MJ.

All good, mostly because all the different looks were clearly frustrating Chase Braggs. Frustrating him at first and then annoying him, Chase starting to force shots and passes. Forcing the *action*, never a good thing for the guy with the ball, the guy who was supposed to be controlling the action.

Not only were the Rams winning the game right now, they had done something Ben thought was impossible:

They had shut up Chase Braggs.

As the Rams came out of a huddle with two minutes left in the half, up twelve points, Coop leaned close to Ben and said, "Pretty quiet from Number 1."

Chase's number. Of course.

"Long way to go," Ben said, what he always said when he felt like one of his teammates was thinking about going into a victory lap *way* too early.

"I'm not an idiot," Coop said. "It's just that we know now that when you're playing like trash you can't talk it."

They held their lead from there until the half. Chase finally hit a jumper, fed Jeb Arcelus for a layup. But Ben made a long two-pointer of his own, the third outside shot he'd made in the half, ended up with the ball again, the Rams with a chance to keep the lead at twelve. Chase guarding him. Waiting for Ben to make his move.

Chase: Almost looking impatient for Ben to get on with it, so the half would be over.

With ten seconds left, Ben dribbled hard to his right, picked up a screen from Shawn, kept going, turned the corner ahead of Chase now, ahead of the play.

Still plenty of time.

"I got him!" he heard Chase yell behind him.

But he didn't.

I got *you*, Ben thought.

As Chase scrambled to get in front of him, Ben crossed

over to his left hand. As he did, Chase Braggs, the great Chase Braggs, got his feet tangled up.

And went down.

Ben didn't waste time checking the shot clock, knew there couldn't be much clock left, pulled up and pushed a soft floater at the basket, saw it go in with three seconds left, the Rams back up by twelve. Chase still on the floor.

Ben reached down to help him up, seeing that Chase didn't want to take his hand, seeing Chase hesitate slightly. But knowing he had to take Ben's hand, knowing how bad he'd look if he didn't. Maybe just not wanting to look bad in front of Lily, whether he cared about everybody else in the gym or not.

Let Ben help him to his feet.

"This isn't over," he said.

"Who said it was?" Ben said.

They went to their benches like fighters going to their corners. Rams 32, Bears 20. Long way to go.

This was one of the times when Coach tried to dial down their excitement a few notches. Like he was trying to pump them down instead of up.

"You gotta understand something," Coach Wright said. "They're too good not to make a run."

Coop said, "We're better than they are today."

Before Coach could say anything Ben said, "For a half."

"Yeah," Coop said, not backing up. "The half we just played and the half we're about to play."

"Hold the thought," Coach said. "But you all gotta go out there with the mind-set that we're down this many points, not up."

Shawn said, "Coach, I heard Jeb say to Chase that this is the most they've been behind all season."

"So now we've got to make sure we keep them down," Ben said.

Ben went to get a drink from a fountain at the other end of the court, giving a quick wave to all the parents: his, Sam's, Coop's, Shawn's. Jeff McBain gave him a quick fist of encouragement back, so quick Ben was sure only he saw it.

On his way back, he tried to lock eyes with Lily, but she was talking away with Molly Arcelus.

But as soon as he did, he slapped the side of his leg, hard, like he was telling himself to snap out of it, stop worrying about Lily and her new Darby friends, just worry about beating the Darby Bears.

The Rams held their lead through most of the third quarter, Coach still mixing and matching with his defenses, making sure to get the guys on the second unit some time in the middle of the quarter, like he always did. It was one of Coach Wright's best things, Ben knew: He played his guys, all of them, no matter how big the game.

It was 44–32, Rams, just over a minute to go in the quarter, both first units back on the court, when the Bears began to make the run Coach had promised they'd make.

Shawn threw a lazy pass to Ben at the top of the key, Chase saw it coming a mile away, picking the ball off, breaking away from what looked like it would be a cheap layup. But Shawn, mad at himself for the giveaway, somehow caught up with him, fouled Chase even as Chase was making the layup. So a two-point giveaway became a three-point giveaway after Chase made the free throw.

Rams up nine now, 44–35.

Darrelle shot way too soon at the other end, way too early in the shot clock, Jeb Arcelus got a long rebound, made a great outlet pass to Chase, who could have taken it all the way to the rim. Instead he pulled up and made a three-pointer and in about ten seconds, the Rams' lead had been cut in half.

Coach yelled, "One shot," at Ben, with thirty seconds left. And they tried to get off the last shot. But Coach Coppo of the Bears had changed some things on his defense, too, had Ryan Hurley playing center now and guarding Coop. The play they wanted to run had Ben throwing a pass to Coop at the free-throw line, but Coop didn't protect the ball well enough, and Ryan was able to punch it loose, to Chase again.

Who got ahead of the pack, pulled up again, made another three.

The horn sounded before Shawn could even get off a heave from halfcourt.

Now the lead was down to three.


The first few minutes of the fourth quarter were pretty much a blur to Ben: Both teams starting to play a little tight now, turning the ball over more than they had in the first three quarters.

MJ fouling out. The crowd loud. Chase in Ben's ear every chance he got, Ben doing his best to ignore that.

Somehow through it all the Rams held on to their lead. Got tied a couple of times, never gave it up, were back up four with ninety seconds left. Bears' ball. There hadn't been much scoring in the quarter, but Chase had done most of it for his team, scoring all but one of their baskets even as Coach Wright kept running different guys at him, still giving him different looks.

"All these different defenses for one guy," he said to Ben at one point. "Wow."

Not acting annoyed any longer, almost acting flattered. Right where he wanted to be. The whole thing about him.

But it didn't matter if the Rams could hold on. Let him be flattered that he'd gotten all this attention on a day his team lost its first game of the season. That's all that would matter, Ben kept telling himself. Not Chase.

Ben was guarding Chase again as he brought the ball down, tried to back Ben closer to the basket. But Ben kept cutting him off, anticipating every move. Finally Chase gave up, took the ball back outside, deep into the shot clock now, wheeled and threw a terrific crosscourt pass to Ryan Hurley — even Ben had to admit it — and Ryan made a short jumper.

Rams up two, 50–48.

Under a minute. Coach told them to play, no time-out, not to worry about the clock, take the first good shot they saw. Ben waved up Shawn for a pick-and-roll, but Chase smothered it. As he did, Ben saw Darrelle come open over in the left corner, one of his hot spots, and Ben threw a pass over to him, over the defense.

Darrelle missed. Another long rebound to Jeb Arcelus. Chase took the outlet in stride, looked like he might try to beat everybody to the basket. Then slowed it down when his coach told him to, pulled it back out.

Forty left.

Coach Coppo called out a play for them. Jeb lost Coop under the basket, Chase saw him, fired a pass in there, for the layup Ben was sure would tie the game.

Only Jeb didn't shoot it. Wasn't the play. With everybody expecting him to, he turned and threw a two-hand, over-the-head pass to Chase in the right corner. Chase down there alone because Ben had thought he was out of the play after the pass to Jeb.

Ben ran straight at Chase, arms up, a step late, his momentum carrying him right out of bounds. He watched from there as Chase's three-pointer went in to put Darby ahead by one.

First time they'd been ahead all day.

Bears 51, Rams 50.

Twenty-two seconds left. Ben's number. Still no time-out from Coach Wright. "Just look for the first good shot," he yelled at Ben. The Bears picked up fullcourt. Shawn inbounded the ball to Ben from under the Bears basket. As Ben turned, Coop showed up to set a killer screen on Chase Braggs, giving Ben a lot of open court, just like that.

Just like that, he was flying down the right side, nobody picking him up right away. Chase did everything for them.

Now he was supposed to make up all that ground between him and Ben McBain.

Only nobody was catching him.

Ryan Hurley came over as Ben crossed the midcourt line, tried to cut him off, Ben dusted him with a crossover move to his left hand. Now he was in the middle of the court, the defense scrambling to catch up to him, to the play.

Jeb Arcelus was the last guy with a chance to get in front of Ben, leaving Coop, yelling, "Pick up my guy," to Ryan as he picked up Ben at the top of the key. Ben slowed down for just a blink, looked away like he was going to pass.

Jeb bit.

The path to the basket looked as wide open as the street in front of Ben's house when he was dribbling toward the basket at McBain Field.

He heard somebody yell from behind him. Chase probably. Pushed off on his left foot for the layup that was going to beat Darby, telling himself not to rush, there had to be plenty of time.

Shot it too hard.

Leaned back from where he ended up under the basket, watched as the ball hit the front of the rim and not the net, watched as it hung there for what felt like about a minute before it fell off, into the hands of Chase Braggs.

Ben knew enough to foul him. Chase went down, as if Ben had fouled him too hard, full of drama — or just himself — to the end. Said, "Hey, I'm not the one who missed the layup." Ben just walked away, watched as Chase walked to the other end of the court and made the first free throw of the one-and-one, then the next.

Darby up three.

Coach did call a time-out then, drew up one of their last-second plays, Coop setting a pick for Ben, Ben going deep, Shawn trying to throw the kind of Hail Mary pass Ben had thrown in football. Only Shawn put too much on it, trying too hard, threw it over Ben's head and right into the hands of Chase, back at the free-throw line, like he was a deep safety in football.

As soon as Chase caught the ball he threw it toward the ceiling, game over, walked right past Ben, saying, "Choker," under his breath as he did.

What happened next depended on which one of them you believed. Or maybe it depended on what you *thought* you saw in the middle of the court at Darby Middle School.

Whether you thought Ben shoved Chase Braggs or not.

What Ben and Chase both knew was that Ben hadn't touched him.

All Ben had said to him was this:

"For a great player you don't even know how to be a good winner."

He'd wanted to say more, a lot more, *plenty* more than that, tell the guy once and for all what he thought about him. But he hadn't. Just that. Great player, lousy winner.

He got up on him as he said it, wanting to make sure only Chase heard him, the way only Ben had heard himself being called a choker.

But that wasn't what Chase wanted everybody in the gym to *see*, even if only he and Ben had heard what went on between them. So he backed away like Ben had bumped him or pushed him, exactly the way guys flopped when they were trying to draw a foul during the game, yelling, "Hey, back off!"

Sam and Coop and Shawn would say later that they hadn't seen what happened, but as soon as they heard Chase, saw there was some kind of scene, they came running across the court to get between them.

"Hey," Chase said, being held back by Ryan Hurley, "tell him to get off me, I wasn't the one who blew the layup."

"What are you talking about?" Ben said. "I was never *on* you."

To his guys Ben said, "I'm fine, nothing happened, the guy's making it up."

Coop was walking him away, anyway, saying, "Chill."

Ben said, "I *am* chill. The only reason I said anything to him was because he called me a choker."

A look came over Coop's face that Ben hardly ever saw, *only* ever saw during a game when he thought someone had cheap-shotted him or one of the other Rams, or crossed some kind of line with chirp or trash talk. "He called you a *what*?" Coop said, and now he started toward Chase until Shawn stepped in front of *him*.

"We gotta get out of this and out of *here*," Shawn said.

They could all hear Chase saying to his own teammates, "All I tried to do was shake the guy's hand and he goes off on me."

Ben shook his head. "Total lie," he said.

But he knew it was a bad scene now, after a bad loss, knew that Chase wanted him to look worse than he had missing the layup that would have won the game.

Why wasn't that enough for Chase Braggs?

*Lily,* Ben thought.

This all had to be for Lily's benefit, he could even see Chase looking up into the stands now to where Lily was frozen in place next to Molly Arcelus, staring out at the court.

Staring at Chase as he pointed to Ben and then to his head, as if Ben had somehow just lost his mind.

The two coaches were there now, then the refs, telling Ben and Chase to cool it right now. The taller of the two refs asked Ben what had happened and he said, "He said something to me, I said something back, that's all."

Chase rolled his eyes and said, "Whatever."

The taller ref said, "*Is* that what happened?"

Chase said, "If he says so, I don't want him to get suspended or anything."

They all knew that a shove didn't get you kicked out of the league the way throwing a punch did. But if one player shoved another, during a game or after it, that player was suspended for a game.

"I didn't do anything to get suspended," Ben said, standing his ground, shaking his head, looking down at the ground so he didn't have to look at Chase Braggs, now a liar on top of anything else. "I just basically called him a jerk. Which he is."

"Right," Chase said. A sneer now where the fake smile usually was. "*I'm* the jerk."

Ben knew he shouldn't have said anything, should just have walked away. Nothing to do about it now. Shawn was right. The only goal now was to get out of this . . . *thing*, get out of the gym, get out of Darby.

The taller ref turned to Coach Wright and said, "Is that what you saw?"

Coach Wright had his arm around Ben, not trying to restrain him, just casual, a way of showing everybody they were standing together.

"Didn't have to," Coach said. "This boy doesn't lie. Ever."

Chase said, "Yeah, right."

Coach Wright made a slow turn of his head now, as if he'd just realized Chase Braggs was standing there. Then he said, "Son, I don't believe I was speaking to you."

Mr. Coppo, knowing his player had crossed the line, walked Chase away from them now, leaning down, talking in his ear, Ben not able to hear what he was saying, just this from Chase when Mr. Coppo stopped talking:

"Not my fault he acted like a loser all over again."

This time it was Sam who started toward Chase, crutches and all. But Ben was the one stopping him now. "Don't bother," he said. "I shouldn't've, either."

"But he's the loser," Sam said.

"Nah," Ben said. "He got everything he wanted. He got the game, he got me missing the layup that would've gotten *us* the game. And on top of that, he makes everybody think I'm the blockhead, not him."

The refs and the two coaches got with each other and had a quick conference, telling the players from both teams to stay where they were. Ben saw Coach Wright shaking his head. They talked a little more. Came back out to halfcourt.

The taller ref said, "It's not like we can do a replay, the way they do in college and the pros. The best thing to do is for everybody to just shake hands and then it's over."

Chase Braggs didn't look too happy about this, but he put out his hand.

Ben looked at it, left him hanging.

Ben McBain said, "No, sir. I can't do that."

"Son," he said, "I'm not gonna suspend you, or write you up. I just want you two to shake hands like good sports."

"I already am a good sport," Ben said. "He's not. I can't shake his hand."

He looked at Coach Wright, saw him smiling as he said to the ref, "Tried to tell you."

Everybody stood there for a moment, nobody saying anything, until Chase Braggs said to Ben, "Now which one of us is a bad sport?"

He and Mr. Coppo walked away. Coach and Ben and the guys did the same. As they did, Ben looked up to where Lily had been sitting.

But she was gone.

Ben rode home with his parents, telling Sam he'd be over later, they were doing the Saturday-night sleepover at Sam's house tonight, the guys all fired up to watch the Bulls play the Heat on television, Derrick Rose against the Heat's Big Three, LeBron and Dwayne Wade and Chris Bosh.

As soon as he was in the backseat, before he even buckled his seat belt, Ben said, "I didn't touch him."

"I know," Jeff McBain said. "I was going to come down and tell everybody that, I saw the whole thing, but then I remembered our deal."

"Don't come on the court unless I'm hurt," Ben said. "And I better be hurt *bad*."

"Your father decided to let you handle it," Beth McBain said from behind the wheel, "whatever *it* was."

"The ref wanted me to shake his hand," Ben said. "I wouldn't do it."

His dad, in the passenger seat, turned all the way around, said, "Really? This guy really did get to you."

"Yeah, Dad, he really did. He called me a choker, even though he wouldn't admit it."

"He said that for real?" Ben's dad said.

"Yeah," Ben said.

Beth McBain said, "And you couldn't walk away this time?".

"No."

"Because this guy has gotten to you," Jeff McBain said.

"Big-time. Somebody that good — and I *know* how good he is, trust me — ought to know how to act. He doesn't."

"And that's all?" his mom said.

They were at a stop sign. He could see her looking at him in the rearview mirror. Calm. Waiting. The way Lily looked at him when she didn't think she was getting the whole story.

Ben thinking in that moment: Lily was the real elephant in the room.

Or this car.

But he didn't want to talk about her right now, especially not with his mom. The best he could do was, "Mom, he started it," knowing how weak that sounded.

"So it was all because of him starting it, and the way the game ended?"

Almost home. It was such a short trip from Darby to Rockwell, but sometimes it felt like they were going cross-country.

"All because I missed a stupid layup!" Ben said, his voice way too loud in the car, and now everything that had happened today, from the time he had missed the layup, the game and Chase and Lily, all of it, just seemed to eat him up all at once, so much that he felt his face getting hot, and his eyes, and thinking that it would be another horrible ending now, him starting to cry. In front of his parents, even from the backseat.

"Hey, bud," Jeff McBain said, his voice soft, turned back around now, maybe seeing what Ben was feeling. "Everybody misses easy ones. You dropped an easy pass that would've won you guys a football game early in the season, and look how the football season turned out."

Ben said, "We could have turned *this* season around today!"

"Sometimes you can just want something in sports too much," his dad said. "And not just in sports, by the way."

Tell me about it.

They were one shot away from being just one game behind Darby in the standings and now look where they were.

Ben went straight upstairs when they got home, closed the door behind him, wondering as he did if Chase Braggs had actually been right about him today. Wondering if wanting something too much in sports was just another way of saying you had choked your brains out.


Ben had a cell phone now, his parents had given it to him a month ago, having given in because so many other sixth graders at Rockwell Middle School had cell phones now.

But he didn't carry it with him all the time, wasn't texting friends every couple of minutes the way so many other kids in his class were, even though when Ben saw the incoming or outgoing texts, he thought they were mostly about nothing.

Sometimes he would text Sam or Coop or Shawn. Or Lily. But mostly if he wanted to talk to them, he'd just call them. And only if he actually had something to say. Ben had promised himself he would never be one of those kids who were checking their phones every minute or so, afraid they would be missing another incoming text about nothing.

One other thing with Ben McBain: He didn't think it was against the law to have an unspoken thought occasionally.

But he texted Lily now. Not just because he felt like he had to explain what she might have thought she saw at the end of the game, but because he wanted to.

Or maybe needed to.

He couldn't let her think he was the jerk. At Pinocchio's, yeah, he had been, everybody heard what he said, everybody knew what happened. Just not this time. He had to make sure she knew what had really happened this time, even if Chase had already given her his version.

**U around? Need to talk to somebody smart.**

And waited.

Waited through dinner, trying to do the kind of phone check with his eyes he hated when he saw other kids doing it, looking down at the phone in his lap when he thought his parents weren't watching, knowing he probably wasn't fooling either one of them.

No message.

No message when his dad drove him over to Sam's for the sleepover, no message back from Lily until Ben was walking up the front walk to Sam Brown's front door.

**Cant help u until u stop acting so dumb.**

He waited until after lunch on Sunday to text her back.

Dumb, she'd said.

Not trying to be funny, that was pretty clear. Not talking about the kind of dumb that meant she was making fun of Ben or somebody else in the Core Four for doing what she called "Dumb Guy Stuff."

Or Extremely Dumb Guy Stuff.

This wasn't about a movie being dumb, or a song, or about dumb behavior from somebody at school.

No.

This time Lily had called Ben dumb and meant it, and that meant she did think he'd acted like a blockhead at the end of the Darby game.

Which meant she *had* gotten another version of it from the real blockhead — Chase — who'd started the whole thing and probably had left out the part about calling Ben a choker.

And Ben couldn't let that go, not even with Lily, *especially* with Lily. Couldn't wait until Monday and school to set the record straight with her once and for all. That was why he texted her now and told her — asked, actually — to meet him at the swings as soon as she could.

If calling him out as dumb was serious, so were the swings at McBain Field.

Those were the swings where their moms had pushed them as soon as they were old enough, the swings where they still went to have their best quiet time and their best talks, when they needed to have a talk.

This time Lily texted him back fast, asked him, like when? Ben's answer went back just as fast.

**Like now.**

She was wearing a Packers hoodie that Ben had given her last Christmas. Ben had ended up with two, his aunt Mary not knowing his parents were getting him one. Green from his parents, yellow from his aunt.

When Lily had told him she liked the green one better, Ben had given it to her on the spot, just like that, saying, "It'll look better on you."

She had said, well, when he put it that way, how could she not accept his generous offer?

Ben was waiting for her at the swings when she pulled up on her bike. And even with everything that had been going on lately, the weirdness, he couldn't help himself, he was happy to see her.

So that much hadn't changed.

"Nice sweatshirt," he said.

Lily said, "I practically stole it off this guy."

Sat down on the swing next to him. As soon as she did, Ben had this flash that the two of them had been sitting right here — together — their whole lives.

"How come you're not watching the Packers?" she said.

"Sunday night game," he said.

She smiled. "Oh, I get it," she said. "You're just killing time with me."

"You know that's not why I asked you to come over," he said, and then didn't mess around, got right to it, saying, "I asked you to come over so I could tell you I'm not dumb."

"Well," she said, still smiling, good sign, "you're going to have to be more specific than that. You're not dumb in general? Or not dumb, like, say, *Pretty Little Liars*?"

It was a show all the girls in their grade were obsessed with, except for Lily, who thought it tried way too hard to be way too scary and wouldn't watch. Or maybe she just didn't want to run with the crowd.

"You pretty much came out and said I acted dumb at the game," Ben said. "But I didn't do anything."

"You didn't shove him?" Lily said.

*"No!"* Ben said, with so much force he was surprised his swing didn't suddenly elevate on its own. "I didn't touch him, Lils."

"All I know is that I saw him go flying backward," she said.

"A flop," Ben said. "Just like guys flop in games, trying to draw fouls."

"Not what he said."

"You talked to him about it?" Ben said. "Before you talked to me?"

Knowing he sounded hurt, not caring.

"He just texted me last night, is all. It wasn't like some case I was trying to crack."

Ben took a deep breath.

147

"In his text," he said, "did he maybe mention that he'd called me a choker?"

Lily was a good enough athlete and knew enough about sports to know what a bad word it was, in any sport.

"No," Lily said.

"Well, he did."

Lily said, "He just said that he tried to tell you that you made their team look like jokers at the end, going past everybody the way you did."

"And you believe that garbage?" Ben said. "I know what he said and I know what I heard."

"What I *really* don't know," Lily said, "is how I ended up in the middle of this." She put air quotes around the last word. "Whatever 'this' is."

In a quiet voice, at quiet McBain Field, nobody else around, no cars on the street, nobody even walking a dog, just Ben and Lily, Ben said, "I didn't think you could be caught in the middle of anything. I just thought it was you and me, like against the world."

"It's *supposed* to be, the way it always has been," Lily said. "Except for the way you've been acting. And I don't just mean yesterday. The way you've been acting practically since the end of football. *That* Ben McBain . . . I don't know the guy."

"But, see, that's the thing, Lils. You're right. Totally. I *was* acting like a dope. But I'm not, anymore. And I wasn't yesterday."

"Hard to tell at the end of the game," she said.

Ben shook his head, looking down at the bare patch of dirt

where his feet were. "He called me a choker for missing the layup," Ben said. "I couldn't let that go. But all I said back was that he didn't even know how to win with class. Then he went out of his way to make me look bad, in front of everybody." Paused and added, "Mostly you."

"We're talking about Chase and *you*," Lily said, her face turned toward him, Ben wondering as always how she could sit cross-legged on a swing and not fall. "This isn't about Chase and *me*."

"Yes," Ben said, his voice quiet as quiet as before, maybe more. "Yes, it is."

"Why?"

"Because he wants to be friends with you the way you and are I friends," Ben said. "And I don't want you to be friends with him like that."

"*That's* what all this is about?" Lily said.

"You're the smartest person our age I know," Ben said. "You're telling me you couldn't see that's what he wants?"

Lily smiled again. "What do you mean the smartest person *our age*?"

Ben said, "So do you?"

"What?"

"Want to be friends with him?"

"I thought I kind of did for a while," Lily said. "But it turns out I didn't know him well enough. But even if he *had* become my friend, he was never going to be the kind of friend to me you are."

In that moment Ben felt like he'd come up for air.

"Doesn't matter now, anyway," Lily said. "I could never like anybody who makes stuff up. Or trust them."

"You believe me, then."

"I always believe you, McBain."

Ben thinking to himself: Get it all out now, before you lose your nerve. You're the one who wanted to have a talk at the swings. So have one.

"Why *did* you like him in the first place?" Ben said.

"Because he was fun, silly," she said. "And he was being fun at a time when you were being no fun at all." She put her feet on the ground, twisted her swing so she was facing him, dead on. "When you *were* acting dumb."

"Maybe," Ben said. "But that guy is a bonehead."

"No, *you* are, for letting this guy get to you from the first day you played against him," Lily said. "You know I'm right, whether you want to admit it or not. Don't even try to deny it."

Ben smiled.

"We're both right," he said. "The guy *is* a bonehead. But this is way more on me than it is on him."

They talked after that, really talked, Ben doing most of it, about how he let Chase get under his skin that first preseason game, how he got so fixed on getting the best of him that he got Sam hurt. How it took him way too long to figure that out. And how he should have been fixed a lot more on getting the best out of himself and his teammates.

Like he always had in the past.

"Wow," Lily said again.

"What?"

"Maybe you're not so dumb after all."

"I was thinking about a lot of this stuff before you showed up today," Ben said. "How much I let it bother me that he's better than me."

"Not so sure about that," Lily said. "Bigger maybe. Not better."

"He is."

"Wasn't yesterday," Lily said. "You guys were great yesterday. *You* were great. You just missed that dumb layup."

"Whatever," Ben said. "But my thing is, I let *all* of it jam me up: his game, the way he chirped on me. And the way he started to hang around you."

She waited, eyes on him, face calm, like they both knew he was finally getting to it now.

Ben said, "All of a sudden a kid I didn't even know a month ago, I was treating him like the most important kid in my world."

"*I* know, Big Ben."

It had been a while since she'd called him that.

"I should've been big enough to walk away yesterday," he said. "But I swear, all I said is what I told you I said."

"I told you. I believe you."

"So we're good?"

"*We* are always good, even when you're doing Dumb Guy Stuff," Lily said. "I want to know if *you're* good."

"Now I am," he said. "I told myself before the Darby game, like, *way* before, that I needed to change my attitude. And as steamed as I was that we lost the game and what

Chase did afterward, when I thought about it, I *had* played that game with a better attitude. My old attitude. I just missed the last shot." Nodded, to himself mostly, and said, "So, yeah, I am good."

"Season's not over, you know."

"Our chance to win the championship is," Ben said.

Lily hit him with her biggest smile of this day now and said, "So?"

"So?"

"So go win the rest of your games and see what happens, you bozo."

Both swings were in the air then, practically at the same moment, both Ben and Lily trying to get as high as they could, trying to outdo each other, the way they always had.

When they finally stopped, they were both out of breath. Ben asked Lily if she had to be anywhere.

"Just here," she said.

Even the practices were great now.

Nobody talked about the record, or looked ahead to the Darby game. The only game they talked about was the next one, this coming Saturday, at home against Hewitt.

The Rams were working harder than ever before, but having fun doing it, the kind of fun you could have in sports without goofing around, everybody on the same page, all of the guys acting almost sad every night when they looked up at the clock and realized practice was over.

Even Sam felt like he was at least part of the action, Coach making sure there was some kind of free-throw shooting contest at the end of practice, Sam able to participate in that. Ben would still seem him grimace if he made too quick a move to pick up a ball, and the doctor said he was still a couple of weeks away from running, but he could stand there and shoot. And even beat everybody some nights.

When they were collecting the balls on Thursday, last practice before Hewitt, Coach came over to Ben and said, "As a coach, you always hope it will happen like this for your team, but you never know."

"Hoping what happens?" Ben said, casually flipping one of the practice balls to Coach behind his back.

"Guys becoming a real team," Coach Wright said. "And I know you know exactly what I'm talking about."

"Believe me, I know," Ben said. "I'm sorry the season is about to end."

"That's something that *does* happen every year," Coach said. "All of a sudden you're closer to the end than the beginning. *Way* closer."

Ben said, "Don't you just hate when that happens?"

"Yeah. But I love coaching my team right now."

"I love playing on it."

"Right now you just love playing *period*," Coach said. "Wasn't so sure about that earlier in the year."

"Same."

"So what changed?"

"Just remembered why I play," Ben said. "And how important it is to me to be part of a team like this."

"Hey," Coach said. "Better late than never."

"Coach," Ben said, "you always say that your goal is for everybody on the team to be better at the end of the season than the start, right?"

"Totally."

"Well, this year I want everybody we *play* at the end to know how much better we got," Ben said. "And to think that even without Sam, we ended up the best team in the league."

Coach smiled now. "Are you sure you're just eleven?"

"Are you serious?" Ben said. "I spent the first half of the season acting like I was *five.*"

Then he said to Coach, "Can I get five more minutes?"

Coach nodded. Ben took a ball out of the rack and dribbled it over and challenged Sam to a free-throw shooting contest.

Sam Brown wasn't back on the court the way Ben wanted him to be, the way Ben had held out hope that he would be from the time he hurt his ankle. But he was moving around so much better now, just a slight limp, down to an ACE bandage wrapping the ankle, carefully shooting around before and after every practice as long as he didn't have to move around too much.

Ben told Sam what he'd just said to Coach, about wanting to finish up looking like the best team in the whole league.

"Dude," Sam said, "trust me on something: I think we already are."

"What about the undefeated Darby Bragging Bears?" Ben said.

Sam reached out, asking for the ball, barely looked as he turned and shot, both of them watching the ball go through the basket without coming close to touching iron.

"Just wait," Sam said.

They went home after that and went to bed and woke up Friday morning finding out they still had a chance to prove they were the best team in the league for real.

That they still had an outside shot of playing themselves into the championship game.

It all had to do with Parkerville losing the night before to a Glendale team that hadn't won a game all season, Robbie Burnett missing the game with the flu. It had to do with that, and the possibility of a tie for second place at the end of the regular season, and tiebreakers.

Even Ben got dizzy trying to explain it to the other guys at lunch. But the bottom line was this: Parkerville now had three losses, Kingsland had three, the Rams had three.

Parkerville vs. Kingsland on Saturday was the last game of the regular season for those two teams, four-thirty on Saturday in Kingsland. If Parkerville won, that knocked out the Rams, because the Patriots had beaten them on that crazy, falling-down shot by Robbie a few weeks ago. Head-to-head matchups were always a tiebreaker, any league.

But:

If Kingsland beat Parkerville and the Rams won their last two games, the Rams would end up tied with Kingsland in second place, *and* would have the tiebreaker on Kingsland, having beaten them on MJ Lau's crazy shot.

Now it sounded crazy to Ben laying this all out for his buds, but the Rams could play Chase Braggs and Darby twice more this season:

Once to end the regular season.

And if they beat them in that one, they'd get them again in the championship game.

"I feel like I'm listening to the announcers trying to explain all the playoff possibilities on the last day of the NFL season," Shawn said.

"I feel like I'm gonna be sick," Coop said.

*"Sick?"* Sam said.

"You know what happens when I start spinning around," he said.

"You want me to go through it all again?" Ben said.

*"No!"* they all shouted at once.

Shawn said, "But this is really happening? We actually still have a shot?"

"We do," Ben said. "And if we beat Hewitt on Saturday, I figure we gotta make a quick road trip to Kingsland to watch them play Parkerville."

"You know what the really sick part of this is?" Coop said. "If we beat Hewitt —"

*"When* we beat Hewitt," Sam said.

"— the Kingsland Knights become our favorite basketball team in the whole world."

After the other guys left, Ben and Sam were still at the table. In a quiet voice Sam said, "Don't tell anybody, but the doc says I can start running in two weeks. Really running. If we make it to the championship game . . ."

Ben said, "Now I like the Knights even better than the Packers."


They nearly didn't make it to Kingsland with a chance.

The Rams were better than Hewitt, by a lot, even without Sam, had a match-up advantage at just about every position on the floor. At least until both their guards, the one Ben was guarding and the one Darrelle Clayton was guarding, decided to pick this particular day and this particular game to start making shots from everywhere except the boys' locker room.

It didn't matter that some of the shots looked like no-look heaves, and a couple of them banked so high off the backboard Ben thought they had actually hit the basket support. They kept going in, enough of them, anyway.

"They're, like, still unconscious," Sam said to Ben during a time-out, early in the fourth quarter, the Rams down by eight points, feeling like they were not just running out of time, but out of season.

"If we don't figure out a way to stop them, we're not just gonna be unconscious," Ben said, "we're gonna be dead. Along with our shot at the championship game."

"Not happening," Sam said.

"And you know this . . . *because*?"

"Because you're not gonna let it happen, that's why."

"You make it sound so simple."

Sam grinned. "Nah, the way they're shooting, it's gonna be really, *really* hard. But that will only make it so much sweeter after you figure it out."

"How?"

Sam shrugged. "Figure it out."

That is exactly what Ben McBain did.

He got Coach to switch him to Darrelle's guy, and Darrelle to switch to his, just to shake things up. And even though they had both been picking their guys up under the Rams' basket, they dogged them even harder now, making them work for every inch, bringing the ball up the court, gambling and going for steals every chance they could, willing to give up fouls if they had to. And even when the Hewitt guards would get the ball over halfcourt, they guarded them even more closely, if that was possible, daring them to drive, taking away any chance at them making the kinds of prayers they had been making all game long.

Trusting that if they did get beat, Coop and Shawn and even MJ would cover for them, making their lives just as miserable if they got anywhere near the basket.

They kept shooting from the outside, though, forcing the shots now, acting shocked when they stopped falling. And when they'd miss again, Coop and Shawn were owning the boards, making outlet passes like pros, starting one fast break after another, Ben in the middle with the ball almost every time.

"Figure it out," Sam had said, and he had, and now it was the Rams who couldn't miss, the Rams who went 16–2 on the Hewitt Giants the rest of the game, the Rams who won the game they needed to stay alive.

The Rams who weren't dead yet.

Coach drove them in his old van: Ben, Sam, Coop, Shawn. And MJ Lau, who'd not only played himself into the starting lineup now, but had become a better all-around player than Ben thought he ever would be, all his hard work somehow dragging his talent along, forcing it to catch up.

One more thing to make Ben feel good about the season, no matter how it ended up:

Coach had asked him to help make MJ a better player, and Ben believed he had, the whole thing starting as simply as possible, Ben showing MJ he wasn't afraid to pass him the ball.

Coach always said that basketball didn't really become a beautiful game until somebody made the first good pass. And somehow that had happened with the first few good passes Ben made to MJ.

No one was ever going to compare him to Kevin Durant as an outside shooter — so far he'd only made three non-layups that Ben could remember — but he wasn't afraid to shoot if

he was open now.

Wasn't afraid, period.

Ben wasn't kidding himself, as well as they had played lately, they weren't nearly as good as they would have been with Sam. Still: They were better than Ben thought they would be, and MJ Lau was a huge part of that.

And now they were walking into Kingsland's small, old-fashioned gym, one that even had a running track up in the balcony, one with hardly any space behind the baskets, the worst lighting in their league, maybe six rows of bleachers, tops, on either side of the court, the place looking to Ben as if it belonged in the movie *Hoosiers*.

None of them cared, it was the only place they wanted to be right now, because this small, old gym held their chance to still make the championship game.

Kingsland needed to beat Parkerville, the Rams needed to beat Darby next week.

Then play Darby the week after that for the title. It was a crazy, outside chance. But all the chance they had.

Coop said, "When was the last time we came to a game we weren't playing?"

They were in the last row of bleachers behind the Kingsland bench, backs against a brick wall.

"Lily," Ben said. "Her championship game in soccer."

"I mean before that," Coop said. "A guys' game."

"Maybe never," Sam said. "But we had to come. Imagine what it would have been like not knowing, waiting to find out."

Both teams were in layup lines. They watched without saying anything until Shawn said to Ben, "What do you really think? About this game?"

"You don't want to hear," Ben said.

Coop said, "Then don't say it."

Ben said, "He asked. It's something Coach always says, about the best player."

Coach Wright nodded, eyes still on the court.

"When everything else looks even," he said, "go with the best player in the game."

"Robbie," Coop said.

"You know what really bothers me?" Sam Brown said. "How different things would be if Robbie didn't make that lucky shot against us?"

MJ said, "You mean like mine against Kingsland?"

"Crazy stuff happens in sports," Coach said. "It's why we play, it's why we watch. Why we care."

"What's really crazy?" Sam said. "We're here."

In the next moment, so was Chase Braggs.


The game clock was running in reverse, under five minutes to the start of the game, when Chase and Jeb Arcelus and Ryan Hurley and Darby's coach, Mr. Coppo, came walking through the double doors behind the Parkerville basket.

"What are *they* doing here?" Coop said.

"Maybe they want to scout these teams in case they play one of them for the championship," Ben said.

"Or," Sam said, "maybe the Brag Man somehow found out we were coming and didn't want to pass up the chance to annoy us."

Coach, who was at the end of the row, leaned toward all of them down, his face serious, like it was a time-out during one of their games and he wanted to make sure he had their full attention.

"No matter what happens today, during the game, after the game, no matter how it comes out, what we do not do with those guys is *engage*," he said. "Got it?"

They all nodded.

"We sit up here, we root quietly, we hope it falls our way in the end," Coach Wright said. "If it doesn't, it doesn't. We walk out of here as a team and remember we've got one more game. Against those guys. And know that we're gonna play it like it's the NCAA finals, even if all we're playing for is pride, and the chance to keep them from going unbeaten."

"Don't worry, Coach," Coop said, grinning. "I'll keep everybody under control."

"Gee, there's good news," Coach Wright said.

The Darby guys sat on the other side of the gym, up behind the Parkerville bench. Ben thinking that it was a lot more fun being them today, knowing they were already in the championship game, knowing it made no difference to them who won today at Kingsland.

Or maybe it did:

Maybe Chase and his boys were on the Parkerville side to root for them. Chase more than anybody. Knowing that if they won the Rams were out of the playoffs.

He knows that if they win, I lose, Ben thought.

He told that to Sam, in a voice just barely loud enough for Sam to hear.

"You're probably right," Sam said. "You know my mom's German, right? There's some fancy word she's always using, one that means that it's not enough for some people to succeed, their enemies have to fail, too."

"I think it should be two words in American," Ben said. "Chase Braggs."

It turned out he had no idea how hard it was to sit and watch a game that meant so much to him, but one he had absolutely no control over, none.

This wasn't anything like rooting for one of his favorite teams in pro sports. Today was different. Oh man, was it. This wasn't just Ben wanting the game to come out right for him. It was much more than that. He wanted it to come out right for Coach, and for his teammates. For Sam, especially. He knew that the Rams weren't any kind of sure thing to beat Darby even if Kingsland won today — heck, they hadn't beaten them yet, not even in the preseason — but he just wanted to have the chance. He wanted to leave this old gym with a chance.

More than anything, he wanted to have some way of controlling the outcome.

Only he didn't.

Ben couldn't will the ball into the basket for the Kingsland Knights, couldn't put rebounds into their hands, couldn't get them a good whistle when they needed one.

He could only watch.

When Robbie Burnett drove the lane right before halftime, scored and got fouled and made the free throw that tied the game, Ben turned to Sam and said, "Watching like this is no fun."

In a low voice Sam Brown said, "Tell me about it."

"Sorry," Ben said. "You know better than anybody."

"Something else I know? It won't get any easier the second half."

"I actually thought about going outside and taking a walk, like I do when it gets tense during a Packers game sometimes."

"Does it ever help?"

"Hardly ever."

"Hey," Sam said, "look at it this way: Game's tied. Coming over here we would have signed up for a tie game at halftime."

"I know," Ben said. "It's still killing me to watch." He turned and looked right at Sam and said, "Did it ever get easier this season?"

"Harder."

"How'd you do it?"

"You're gonna laugh," Sam said. "But I kept telling myself they're just games."

"And you waited all this time to tell *me*?" Ben said.

"And the whole time, my dad kept telling me that if spraining my ankle and missing one season is the worst thing that ever happens to me in sports, well, I'm good."

Ben put his fist out, Sam bumped it. Ben said, "Yeah, you're good."

Every once in a while during the second half, Ben would look over to where Chase and the Darby guys were sitting. Sometimes they weren't even watching the game, other times they were talking and laughing, like this was a game on television and they were in the room, but only about half paying attention to it.

Don't get mad at them, Ben told himself.

It doesn't matter to them the way it matters to us.

To me.

The game was still tied going into the fourth quarter, Ben having given up hoping that Kingsland would go off on a rip, put some distance between them and the Patriots, build up a ten- or twelve-point lead, just so he didn't have to keep hanging on every possession and every shot.

No such luck. Not that kind of game. Nobody had been ahead by more than four points from the start.

And when somebody finally did pull away, it was the wrong team.

Best player, wrong team.

In the end Robbie Burnett won the day the way Ben had been afraid he would, taking down the Knights, taking down the Rams at the same time. Not a thing Ben could do about it, or his coach, or any of his teammates. Just had to sit there and watch it play out the way it did, nobody able to stop Robbie, the game in his hands, the ball in his hands, a great player playing himself and *his* teammates past the Kingsland Knights and into the championship game.

It started when he made a three, just under four minutes

left. Then came a steal, and a breakaway layup. A Kingsland miss, and then another three.

Parkerville by eight, just like that, Ben feeling as if the whole thing had happened in a few seconds.

Kingsland tried to run its offense, get a good shot, did get one, an open look for their center. Who missed. Robbie came down, dribbled off some clock, got fouled finally, made two free throws.

Parkerville by ten, two minutes left.

"Still time," Coop said, as if he thought he had to say something.

"No," Ben said. "There's not. They're done, we're done."

Kingsland didn't score again until right before the horn. Parkerville 42, Kingsland 30. All the time Ben had been thinking and stressing on Chase Braggs this season and Robbie had done just as much to knock them out of the championship game, done it with his crazy shot against Ben and the Rams, done it by taking charge this way against the Knights.

The difference between him and Chase was that Ben liked Robbie Burnett, which is why when the game ended, he was right there to shake his hand, tell him great game, wish him luck against Darby in a couple of weeks.

"You beat those guys," Ben said.

"Gonna try," Robbie said, shoulder-bumped Ben before he walked off.

When Ben turned around, Coach was standing there, saying, "What do you say we blow this town?"

"Fine by me," Ben said.

Chase Braggs and the Darby guys were standing by the double doors, waiting while Mr. Coppo congratulated some of the Parkerville players. Coach Wright and the rest of the Rams walked past the Darby kids with nods, just wanting to get out of there, Ben just slowing down long enough to say hey to Ryan Hurley, a guy he'd always liked from football.

As he did, Chase managed to get between Ben and the doors.

"Do not engage," Coach had said.

Chase said, "Tough one for you guys, huh?"

Ben shrugged. "We put ourselves in this position."

He tried to go around Chase, but Chase Braggs took a step to his right, not making a big show of what he was doing, but doing a great job of cutting Ben off, like Ben was making a move to the basket and not the parking lot.

"Lily told me what you said about me," Chase said. "Well played."

"Wasn't playing anybody," Ben said. "Just telling the truth. Listen, I gotta bounce."

Chase wasn't done.

"Must be tough for you, not making the championship game, everybody says you almost always win at everything."

"Nobody does in sports," Ben said.

"I do," Chase said.

And Ben couldn't help himself now, he laughed.

"What's so funny?" Chase said.

"Lot of stuff, actually," he said. "Listen, our team does have a championship game. Next Saturday. Against your team.

And after we win it, you're gonna have to ask yourself a question."

"Really?" Chase said. "Like what?"

"Like what would have happened between our teams this season if the sides had been even," Ben said.

Then he was out the door, out to where Sam was waiting outside. They'd all lost a chance at the championship game today. Sam had lost his chance to just *play* this season.

Before Ben could say anything, Sam said, "Least I had a shot, dude. All you can ask for is a shot."

Still the best player on the team, even now.

Lily came by for breakfast: Chocolate-chip pancakes that she made for both of them, two huge stacks when she was done, as if she was fueling up for the Darby game right along with him.

When they had cleaned up, Lily said, "You good to go?"

"I am," Ben said.

"For real?"

"For real, Lils. I can't wait to play this game."

"It's not the kind of last game you thought you'd be playing against them."

"Nope," he said. "Not gonna lie. I wanted to play them for the championship. But it's like I've been saying all week, and Coach has, and everybody: This *is* our championship game. I don't think Parkerville has a chance to beat them in the real championship game, but I think we can."

"Will that be enough?" Lily said, just the two of them, her on one side of the kitchen table, Ben on the other, Lily wearing her lucky "Big Ben" T-shirt, the one with the famous London clock on the front. "You wanted to take them down pretty bad all season."

"Now I want it just as much," he said. "But in a good way. Not just because we can be the ones to knock them out of an undefeated season. Because if we beat them today, without Sam, we have the right to walk away thinking that if the sides had been even, our best would have been better than theirs."

Lily smiled. "I don't want to pop your balloon, but it's not like they have a whole lot to play for today."

"You're wrong," he said. He smiled. "I know that hardly ever happens, but you're wrong. They're gonna want to rub our faces in it one more time today. And Chase is gonna want to stick it to me in front of you. No lie, Lils, I think he might be more pumped for this game than he will for the real championship game."

"This is the most excited you've been about basketball since Sam got hurt."

"It's 'cause I *am* excited," he said. "Here's the thing: All along Coach told me I had to make the other guys better. Said that's my real job, what I do. And I said I understood, but it took me all year to *actually* understand. For me to stop acting like a bonehead."

"You?" she said. "A bonehead? I must have missed that *totally*."

"Ha-ha," he said. "And that's not even the best part of the whole thing."

"And that would be?"

"I made myself better."

"Got a feeling we're not just talking about hoops."

"No," Ben said, "we're not."

"But you still want to beat Darby," Lily said.

"As Coach likes to say, like a rented mule."

He called Sam and asked if he wanted a ride to the game, but Sam said he wasn't ready yet, he'd see him there. So it was Ben and Lily in the backseat, Ben's dad driving them, Jeff McBain observing that this was pretty early for Lily to be getting to the gym.

"I want to walk in with Ben," she said.

"I always think of it as me walking in with *her*," Ben said.

"So this is one of those Ben and Lily things," Ben's dad said.

"Lily and Ben," she said.

"Sorry."

"Plus," she said, "with a game this big, I wanted to get my game face on as soon as possible."

"Game face?" Ben said. "You sound like one of the guys."

"There's no reason to be mean," she said.

As early as they were getting to the gym, Shawn and Coop and MJ were already there, out on the court, shooting around. When Ben joined them Coop said, "Straight up? I don't want this season to end."

"Same," Ben said.

Shawn said, "So we figured the earlier we got here, the more we could stretch out the day."

MJ Lau grinned. "I finally learn to shoot and *now* we have to stop playing?"

Ben grabbed a ball out of the rack, rolled it around in his hands, then cradled it in his right hand and flicked his wrist and shot it straight up in the air with perfect rotation. Just getting the feel.

"So let's just make this the best day of the whole season," he said. "Because it's gonna have to last us until baseball."

"You're telling me that with snow still on the ground," Coop said. "Now I feel worse than ever that the season is ending."

"But think how good you're going to feel if we beat Chase Braggs," Ben said.

Shawn said, "I heard he's been telling everybody that beating us three times this season will be as sweet as beating Parkerville."

"So what?" Coop said. "He's already organizing a victory parade down Main Street in Darby? Like the ones New York teams get when one of their teams wins a championship?"

"Hey," Ben said, "this isn't only about him today. Shoot, I made way too much of the season be about him. This is about us. Our team. The team we made ourselves into."

The rest of the Rams began to show up. The day none of them wanted to let go of began to take shape. The bleachers slowly began to fill up, parents and relatives from both towns, kids from both schools. It wasn't a championship Saturday, but it was still a big-game Saturday, because it was Rockwell vs. Darby. Coach Wright came walking through the double doors, chatting with the two refs. Coop's dad was at the scorer's table, testing the clock, and then the horn, Coop's dad loving the job of running the clock because he said it kept him a lot calmer during games than he'd be sitting in the stands.

Darby's players showed up about forty-five minutes before the game was supposed to start, Chase leading them into the gym, of course. As soon as he was inside, Ben saw him looking over to the Rockwell side of the gym, trying to see if Lily was already here. When he spotted her, he waved, but as he did, Lily managed to pick that exact moment to turn and say something to Ben's mom.

Lily wasn't sitting with Molly Arcelus today, she was sitting with Ben's parents. Now Ben looked back at Chase, who quickly pulled down his arm, Ben smiling as he thought: Shame to see a brother left hanging like that.

Good beginning to the day. One Ben McBain was convinced would end up being a great day, this powerful feeling he had that they were going to do it, finally, they were going to stop the Darby Bears.

That their best would be better today.

No eye contact with Chase, none, as the scoreboard clock continued to run down to the zeroes that would eventually mean the game was ready to start. Ben just concentrated on making his layups when he was still in the layup line — if it came down to a layup today, he wasn't missing this time, not on a bet — and then his outside shooting.

Practice with a purpose, Coach always said. Practice like you play.

And, man oh man, he couldn't wait to play. In sports you always heard about somebody being the team to beat. Well, there that team was at the other end of the gym, once and for all. Team to beat. The one nobody had beaten all season. One more time, Ben told himself he was playing for the championship of that. Whether the season was ending too soon or not, he was going to do everything and give everything to make sure it ended right.

He looked up at the clock.

Under five minutes to the start of the game.

He felt ridiculously excited.

But not nearly as excited as he was when the double doors at the other end of the gym opened up when Sam Brown came running through them.

Sam Brown in his white home jersey, No. 23 to Ben's 22, sprinting by the Rams' bench as Coach fed him a perfect bounce pass, Sam dribbling the ball toward his teammates, smiling, driving right past Ben and Coop and Shawn, laying the ball in.

Ready to play.

After the layup, Sam ran over to where Ben was standing,
mouth still wide open.

Ben said "What . . . ?"

Sam was still smiling. "Am I doing here?"

"Pretty much."

Sam said, "Same thing as you. Getting ready to give Darby
a beatdown."

Then he explained to all of them, talking as fast as he
could, the game really about to start now: How only Coach
knew there was a chance he could play today, that he'd made
more progress this week than anybody thought he would, his
parents included, and had started running this week instead of
next. Said he didn't want anybody else to know — not even
his boys — that this might happen, just in case it didn't.

So he'd been working out on his own, in his driveway, all
week. Even as late as yesterday, when the doc took one more
set of X-rays, gave him one more round of range-of-motion
tests, he said he'd need to see Sam this morning before he
cleared him to play. See him run as hard as he could, and do it

176

without pain. He and Sam and Sam's parents had used the big gym at Rockwell High School, made him do stops and starts, go end to end, even jump for rebounds on shots his dad was missing on purpose.

The reason the workout had started so late was because another one of the doc's patients had picked that morning to fall and break a hip.

"I can't believe this," Ben said. "You've never been able to keep a secret your whole life."

"But my first one didn't stink, right?"

Coach was with them now on the court, saying, "I thought that if anything could get us fired up more for this game than we already were, it would be Sam running through those doors."

"Basically," Sam said, "we thought it would be a pretty cool way for our season to end. And mine to start."

Sam shot a couple of more quick layups, Ben feeding him, then had time to shoot a few free throws and a few jumpers from the wing before the horn sounded. Then the Rams — all of them now — walked toward their bench. Coach saying, "I thought about trying to have Sam get one practice in, but then he reminded me of something."

Sam said, "After having to sit and watch all season, I know our plays better than he does."

"In my whole life," MJ Lau said, "I've never been happier to give up my spot."

"You don't have to," Coach said. "We start the same five we've been starting. Don't worry, I'll get Number 23 in there soon enough."

One of the refs came over and said, "Ready to start the game, Coach."

Coach made a sign, like one minute. Put his hand out. The others came in on top of it.

"I've been telling you guys that we're more a team than I ever thought we were going to be," he said. "Well, guess what? Now we're even more team than that."

He was kneeling. Looked up now.

"Anybody got anything to add?" he said.

"Yeah," Ben said. "The sides are finally even."


But the other side was still the Darby Bears who hadn't tricked anybody on the way to winning all their games, even if Ben had helped them stay undefeated by missing a layup along the way.

And as obnoxious as Chase Braggs was — *still* was, holding his follow-through after making his first outside shot, on his team's first possession — he could really play and his team could really play.

But so could the Rockwell Rams.

It was 10–10 when Coach put Sam into the game, halfway through the first quarter. Ben and Chase had been guarding each other up until then, each having scored three baskets already. But as soon as Sam was on the court, he came over to Ben, grinning.

"You guard Jeb for a few minutes," he said. "I'll take Mr. Wonderful."

"I'm thinking he won't have quite the same size advantage on you as he does me," Ben said.

"Guess what?" Sam said. "You're not the only one who wants a piece of that guy. I just waited longer to get mine."

"Make it a big one."

Sam missed his first shot, rushing it, too ramped up, almost trying to get the ball through the hoop before he even released it. But somehow Ben outfought all the big guys for the rebound, turned, and threw it right back out to Sam.

Who didn't hesitate, shot almost the same shot he'd just missed.

Drained this one.

Ben couldn't help himself, pumping his fist as he ran back up the court, feeling as if it was the biggest assist he'd gotten all season.

Chase looked surprised when he saw Sam guarding him, Sam picking him up in the backcourt, pressing him like he was trying to force a steal in the last minute of the game and not the first quarter, making him fight hard just to get the ball into the frontcourt before there was a ten-second violation. But once he made it, Ben knew that Chase wasn't going to run a play for Jeb Arcelus now, or Ryan Hurley. He was going to show Sam right away he could get his shot on him the way he did everybody else.

Ryan set a high screen for him, but Sam jumped it, almost like Ryan wasn't there. Staying right with Chase as he turned and started to back Sam toward the basket.

Going right to his go-to move.

Backing Sam in for a turnaround.

Ben watched as Chase head-faked one way, then the other. Sam didn't go for either one, didn't bite, looked completely calm even as he gave ground, almost like he wanted Chase to get to his spot.

When Chase was close enough, he gave one more little shake of his head, turned, and went into his shot. Sam was ready for it, timing Chase's release perfectly, using his own length on Chase Braggs now, blocking the shot so hard it went rocketing into the bleachers. Telling Chase in that moment what guys always told shooters who got a shot smacked like that, whether they actually said anything or not:

Get that weak stuff out of here.

Sam Brown never changed expression. Just waited for the ref to hand Chase the ball so he could inbound it. When the ref did that, Ben heard Chase say, "He got my hand."

The ref smiled.

"Not unless your hand had 'Wilson' written across it, son," the ref said. "That was what we like to call all ball."

For the rest of the first half, that's what the Rockwell-Darby game was: All ball. Good, hard, serious ball. Coach let Sam play out the first quarter, then sat him back down, seeing how winded he was. You could play all you wanted in your driveway but playing in a game was totally different, especially if you'd been sitting on the bench all year the way Sam had. It was like the first day of practice when you scrimmaged hard for the first time, and wondered if you were going to be able to catch your breath ever again.

Between quarters Sam said, "You know how you always tell me how the game slows down for you?"

They talked about it all the time, how when you felt like you were in control of the action, it was as if everybody else in the game was moving in slow motion.

"Yeah," Ben said.

"When's that gonna happen for me today?"

"When you get back out there," Ben said. "You're back in it now, dude. When you get back out there again, you'll feel like you haven't missed a game. Trust me."

"Always," Sam Brown said.

Ben went back on Chase to start the second quarter. But Chase got hot, making three straight shots. The last one was a great drive in traffic, Chase beating Ben off the dribble, then blowing right past Coop when Coop tried to cut him off.

It was 24–18, Darby now. As Chase ran up the court, he leaned close to Ben and said, "You *still* can't guard me."

Ben ignored him. But as soon as he was in the frontcourt he crossed over *hard* on Chase, right hand to left hand in a flash. Only just as Chase leaned to his left, Ben immediately crossed *back* over on his dribble, and when Chase tried to cover that, his feet got tangled and he went down. In the clear now, Ben went straight up the middle, forced Ryan Hurley to pick him up, making a sweet feed to Shawn as he did, Shawn laying the ball in.

Didn't say a word to Chase as he ran past him, didn't look at him, just shrugged, like the whole thing was no big deal.

Sam came back in with two minutes left in the half. Game tied now. This time Ben stayed on Chase, who missed a fallaway the next time the Bears had the ball. Coop rebounded the ball and made his outlet pass to Ben almost in the same motion, and suddenly Ben and Sam were out on the break.

Two-on-one.

Their two against Chase's one.

Ben was on the right, Sam to his left, good spacing between them, Chase backing up. As Ben got into the lane, Chase made his move on defense, backing off, sure Ben was going to feed Sam.

And he *was* going to feed Sam, had committed to passing him the ball, had it in his right hand. Only now Chase was there, so all Ben could do, having given up his dribble, was try a shot he hadn't tried all year. Or practiced, even at McBain. Or knew he even had. A one-handed scoop shot from about ten feet away from the basket, a floater, like a reverse teardrop.

Nothing but net.

Now the Rams were ahead by a basket, stayed ahead by a basket until the half, Rams 30, Bears 28.


Coach did something he hadn't done all season, took them off the court at halftime, into the boys' locker room, Gatorade and water bottles waiting for them in there, telling them to take a seat on the benches.

"I'm not gonna tell you the second half is our season," he said. "Because it's *not* our season. I'm too proud of everybody in this room to say that nothing else that happened before this game mattered. It mattered a lot. I'm as proud of this team and the way it's battled as any team I've ever coached."

He wasn't making a speech here, wasn't raising his voice, was just talking to them, not just about basketball.

"Lot of challenges from the start," he said. "From inside our team and out. But no matter what happened, we hung together. And got better. And kept fighting. As a coach? All you can ever ask."

Coach smiled. "Not only did we get a player back today we thought we'd lost for the season, we found another player — in MJ — while Sam was gone. So now there's one more good player in Rockwell."

Knock on the door then, the taller of the two refs poking his head in. "Keith, the other team's already out there warming up. You got about five minutes."

Coach thanked him, said they'd be right out, turned back to the Rams. "These last two quarters, this isn't just where we're supposed to be. It's where we want to be. This isn't about just giving them their first loss. It's about us getting one more win."

Then he walked past his players, one by one, pounded each one of them some fist.

"Let's go beat those guys," he said.

The Rams ran out of the locker room yelling, got back on the court with three minutes left before the start of the second half.

First thing Ben saw when he got out there was Chase talking to Lily, who was standing behind where Mr. Manley sat at the scorer's table. When Chase saw that the Rams were back on the court, he walked away, shaking his head.

Ben told himself to wait until after the game to find out what all *that* was about, until he saw Lily waving him over, telling him to hurry.

"Wondering what we were chatting about?" she said. Smiling.

"Chatting?" Ben said.

"Whatever," Lily said. "He told me that he was glad Sam was back, because now you guys wouldn't have any excuses when they beat you again."

"Now he's chirping on *you*?"

"Pretty much."

"So what'd you tell him?"

Lily said, "I told him he just better watch out for Number 22."

"He didn't look too happy walking away."

"The last thing he said was that you still couldn't guard him," Lily said.

"Yeah, he might've mentioned that to me in the first half."

Lily said, "Then I told him this was going to be the day when it was the other way around." She reached across the scorer's table, gave Ben a high five, said, "So don't make a liar out of me, big boy."

He had time to shoot a couple of layups in the line, then a few free throws, saw Coach telling him to get over to the bench. When he got with the guys, Coach said, "I'm gonna start Sam, bring MJ off the bench to give us a jolt about halfway through the quarter."

Turned to Ben.

"You want me to have Sam start out on Chase?"

Ben shook his head, no. Emphatically.

"I got this," he said.

"Works for me," Coach Wright said.

And Ben said to him, to all of them, "I've been waiting all season for this."

Coach sat Ben about halfway through the quarter, telling him he better get his rest now, because once he went back in the only way he was coming out was if *he* was the one who sprained an ankle.

When Coach did put him back in, minute and a half left in the third quarter, the Bears had gone ahead by four, having just run two clean fast breaks in a row, Chase the finisher on both of them.

But then Coop made one of two free throws and Ben fed Sam for his first three-pointer of the season with thirty seconds left. Game tied.

Bears with the last shot of the quarter.

Chase held the ball all the way out near halfcourt, ball on his hip, eyes on the shot clock, clearly loving the moment, knowing all the other eyes in the gym were on him.

Ben laid off him, maybe six feet, waiting for him to make his move.

186    Him and Chase Braggs.

Chase started dribbling with twelve seconds left, Ben knowing because he could see the shot clock at the other end. But as Chase started to his right, Sam Brown left Jeb Arcelus, and ran right at Chase, waving his arms like a crazy person, like he was about to tackle him, or just run him over.

The moment was weird enough to throw Chase off *just* enough, got him looking at Sam instead of the guy guarding him. Ben. Who flashed in front of Sam, between Sam and Chase, and took the ball away, as if it had gone from Chase's dribble to Ben's.

Ben was at full speed right away, allowing himself one quick look at his own shot clock. Five seconds now. Plenty of time to get a layup. A wide-open layup he didn't plan to miss this time against Darby.

Got his stride just right as he closed on the basket, pushed up off his left foot, ready to put his team up by a basket, *this* basket, going into the final quarter. Final quarter of the whole season.

Ready to do all that until he got hit from behind.

Got knocked out of the air, sent flying and spinning into the wall behind the basket, missing the padding, hitting the door frame, hitting it hard with the back of his right shoulder. Going down hard.

Looking up to see that the only person who could have put him down this way was the Darby Bear closest to him.

Chase Braggs.

A lot going on then, mostly with Ben's right shoulder, so much pain shooting through it Ben was afraid to even try to raise his right arm, afraid to make the pain even worse.

And here came Sam and Coop and Shawn, all of them running toward Chase, as if in a race to see who could get to him first.

Ben could see Coach running, too, but he was behind the action. Ben had to get up and get between his guys and Chase before something stupid happened.

Ben got there just in time, put up his left arm, his good one, telling them to stop, like he'd turned himself into a school crossing guard.

It worked, but they weren't happy about it.

Coop yelled at Chase, "Nice cheap shot, dude. Really nice."

Chase put his own hands up, like, hey, he hadn't done anything wrong. "Hard foul, is all," he said. "Trying not to give up a three-point play."

Sam had stopped, but he wasn't happy about it. "I'd call it a flagrant foul," he said, glaring at Chase. "But it was actually dirtier than that."

"You don't know basketball, then," Chase said, not backing off, chirping to the end.

"Know you, though," Sam said.

The refs came in, the taller one moving Chase away, the shorter one shooing Sam and Coop and Shawn toward the Rams' bench. Both refs saying the same thing: "Enough."

Coach was with Ben, asking if he was all right. Ben lied, said he was. The refs got together, decided it *was* a flagrant foul, that Chase hadn't made any attempt to make a play on

the ball.

Two free throws for Ben, Rams kept possession, three seconds still showing on the clock.

Just one small problem, as Ben saw it.

He knew he couldn't shoot the free throws, his shoulder still felt as if Chase had hit him from behind with a shovel.

Couldn't shoot them but *had* to. Couldn't let anybody on the court, certainly not the guy who'd sent him flying, know how much he was hurting. And Ben knew the rules, knew that if he couldn't shoot his own free throws the Darby coach, Mr. Coppo, could pick anybody the Rams had, whether he was in the game or not, to shoot them for him.

Sam knew something was wrong, just because he was Sam, and could see when something was wrong with Ben the way Lily could.

"You okay?"

"Perfect."

"No, you're not," Sam said. "You just hit that wall like a race car."

"I'm good."

Sam gave him a long look. "Can you shoot?"

Somehow Ben managed a grin. "Better than you," he said.

Wanting to make these two free throws more than any two he'd ever attempted in his life. Walked toward the line, casually trying to raise his right arm, like he was stretching.

Stopped halfway up.

He was starting to wonder if he could get the ball to the basket left-handed, or just tell Coach the truth, when he came up with a better idea.

He'd shoot them *Hoosiers* style.

The way he shot them for fun at McBain.

Just for real this time.

Ben took the ball from the ref, bounced it a couple of times, reminded himself not to let his right hand, his dominant hand, try to do too much. Not that there was much chance of that at the moment.

Took a deep breath. Maybe looked for all the world like he was going to shoot regulation, then just dropped his hands to the sides of the ball, underhanded it toward the basket with a flick of both wrists.

Like Ollie had in the movie.

"What the heck?" he heard somebody behind him say as the ball just glanced across the front of the rim, hit softly off the back, dropped through.

When the second one hit nothing but string, the Rockwell fans exploded the way the fans of Hickory High had when Ollie made his free throws in the movie.

Sam inbounded the ball after that, Shawn got a pretty good look at a three, just missed it, horn sounded, the Rams walked toward their bench with a two-point lead, 42–40.

Between Ben and the bench was Chase Braggs, still staring at him, Ben sure he knew why, because of the free throws.

For once, Chase didn't say anything.

But Ben did, he couldn't help himself, smiling despite the pain behind his shoulder, saying to Chase, "Dude, what, you're the only one who can style?"

The job now, Ben knew, was convincing Coach that as hard as he'd banged his shoulder it was only a temporary stinger, that's why he'd shot the free throws Ollie-style, that he didn't need to come out of the game, that he was feeling better already.

Only Coach wasn't buying it, telling him to sit down, putting an ice pack to the back of Ben's shoulder and holding it there.

"Coach, I'm fine."

"No, you're not."

"I am *not* sitting this out!" Ben said.

"Relax," Coach said. "I'm not asking you to. We're gonna keep this ice on it for a few minutes."

"No!" Ben said.

*"Yes,"* Coach said. "You're gonna sit here next to me and then when we take the ice off, you're going to tell me the truth about whether you think you'll hurt us more or help us if I put you back in. Okay?"

Ben knew it wasn't really a question.

"Okay," he said, reaching across his body with his left hand, showing Coach he could hold the ice pack himself.

Telling himself as he did that Chase Braggs, the guy who'd been finding ways all season to knock him down, was not going to knock him out of this game — out of the season — for good.

Once the fourth quarter started, Ben told Coach about every thirty seconds he was good to go. "Soon," Coach kept saying. Finally, five minutes left, Ben feeling like about five lifetimes had passed, game tied, Coach turned to Ben and said, "Okay, kid: Show me what you got."

Ben put the ice pack down, stood up, not sure what was about to happen, not sure if it was just the ice that made his shoulder feel better. But with Coach Wright watching him, he stood up, put his right arm straight up in the air, smiling through the pain he felt as he did. Like it was no big deal.

Then he made a shooting motion, even holding his pose the way Chase did.

"I'm good, Coach."

Coach smiled at him and said, "Actually, you're quite a bit more than that."

And told him to get in there for MJ on the next whistle.

There were four minutes, thirty seconds left when the next whistle came, Ben signaling to MJ that he was coming in for him, Darby ahead 47–45, guys on both teams starting to drag just a little bit, just because the game to here had been so intense, the Darby Bears playing this one as if it meant as much to them as it did the Rams.

Sam came right over to Ben and said, "I'd give you a slap on the back but, well, you know."

"Here's what I know," Ben said. "We're not losing this game."

Things had gotten ragged at the start of the fourth quarter, stayed ragged now, nobody scoring the first two minutes Ben was back out there. He still hadn't taken a shot from the outside, no good looks for him yet. But he kept telling himself that the first time he *did* get a good look, he couldn't hesitate.

Didn't hesitate when Sam swung it over to the left wing and Ben was wide open from fifteen feet.

Air ball.

It wasn't so much the grab he was still feeling behind the shoulder. His arm just felt stiff. Weak. At a time when the other guys in the game weren't getting much push from tired legs, Ben had no push in his arm, knew that if he was scoring the rest of the game, he was doing it by driving the ball.

He drove it the next time the Rams had the ball, just decided to put his head down when he saw an opening and go for it, faked a pass to Sam, drove to his left, made a left-handed layup to tie the game at 47.

"Lefty?" Sam said. "Seriously?"

Ben got close to his ear and said, "Seriously? I had no choice."

It was hurting him now, he knew, just to dribble the ball with his right hand. Nothing to do about it. He was going to play through it now, use his left hand more if he had to. He wouldn't have ever said this to Coach, but he believed that even hurt like this, he was still the best point guard his team had.

And he knew that Chase knew his game well enough by now to know that he had to honor Ben's left hand, especially now that he'd scored with it.

Chase drove the ball at the other end, got fouled, missed the first free throw, made the second. Darby, 48–47. Minute and a half left. That much season left for the Rams. Shawn missed a wide-open three, Jeb Arcelus rebounded, fed Chase, who threw it ahead to Ryan Hurley for a layup. Darby by three.

One minute, straight up.

Ben had the ball at the top of the key. Coop came out and set a screen for Shawn to Ben's right, Ben eyeballing both of them all the way, waiting for Sam to do what Ben had told him to do as they came up the court:

Make a perfect back-door cut from the left corner, Ben seeing the flash of white and lobbing a pass over the defense at the same moment, Sam catching it in perfect stride, catching it and laying it in, same motion, back to being the kind of athlete who could do that now.

Back to being Sam.

Bears 50, Rams 49.

Fifty seconds left.

"No fouls," Coach shouted at them.

They were going to play it out, try to get a stop, get the ball back. Even if the Bears ran the clock all the way down before shooting, the Rams would have fifteen seconds, plenty of time to set up the last shot of their season.

Even if the Bears scored — anything except a three, anyway — the Rams would still have time to make a three of their own and send the thing into overtime.

Sam had been guarding Chase. Ben told him to switch, that he'd take him. "You sure?" Sam said.

"I have to," Ben said.

Sam said, "Yeah, you do."

Chase crossed halfcourt, kept his dribble, Ben giving him room, Chase finally going to his right with thirty seconds left, the other Bears clearing out for him.

Him against Ben.

Had to be, Ben thought. Had been the two of them all year. Ben watched Chase's dribble, telling himself he couldn't go anywhere without the ball. Knowing there was no way Chase was giving it up.

But instead of guarding him close, Ben backed up now, all the way off him, ten feet of air between them at least. Daring him to shoot right now. Remembering what Sam had told him that night at McBain before he hurt his ankle. About Chase pounding the ball hard right before he went into his shot. Chase did that now, and as he did, *now* Ben ran at him, arms up, getting as close as he could without fouling him or even touching him.

Chase missed.

Not by a lot. But the ball was wide right all the way, just enough, catching the side of the rim, Sam outjumping the world for the rebound.

Twenty left.

Sam kicked it to Ben as Coach yelled, "Go!" Telling them that he wasn't calling that last time-out, just to push the ball and go get a good shot.

Like he was telling them to go win the game.

Ben pushed it up the right side, Sam cutting behind him, Ben saying, "Back door again," just loud enough for Sam to hear. Ben telling himself not to rush, that there was plenty of time to have the play work again.

Only Shawn and Coop were over on the left side this time, Sam's side of the court, and so was Darrelle. It was why it must have looked to everybody in the gym as if the Rams had cleared out the right side for Ben against Chase, even thought they really hadn't.

Ten seconds.

Chase overplayed him on the right, knowing Ben was hurt, having to know. Ben spun away from him, back to the basket, trying to count down in his head. Still hoping to see some flash of white, Sam or somebody else, somebody he could pass to before it was too late.

"Five!" Coop yelled.

No time to face up now, no time to do anything but try to make a turnaround against Chase, even with the height advantage Chase had.

Ben spun and all he could see was those long arms in front of him.

Telling himself that he just had to raise his right arm one last time in the basketball season.

Letting the ball go, ignoring the pain, telling himself to shoot it as high and hard as he could. Later, when he pictured the shot in his head, before he even looked at the video his mom had taken, he'd think of the ball falling all the way out of the rafters.

Maybe that's why it hit the net as softly as it did, maybe that's why the ball went through as cleanly as it did, Chase turning and seeing what the whole gym did before they all heard the horn, seeing that Ben had made the rainbow turnaround fallaway that beat Darby, 51–50.

Chase Braggs saw all that, then saw the ball bounce harmlessly away, before he turned and stared at Ben.

Mouth closed for once.

For one quick moment, there and gone, Ben thought about telling him, "*You* can't guard *me*."

But he didn't.

He just ran for Sam, because Sam was the closest one to him, and gave him a flying chest bump.

Feeling no pain before he went looking for Lily.

"You're hurt," she said, standing on the court in front of the Rams' bench. "I knew as soon as you hit the wall, before you shot the free throws like that kid in your movie."

"My dad's got this expression he says he stole from some old tennis coach," Ben said. "If you're hurt, you don't play. If you play, you're not hurt."

Lily shook her head. "Guys," she said. "Even smart guys like your dad. You can find reasons to justify everything."

Ben smiled. "No pain, no gain," he said.

Lily shook her head again and then said, "Another dopey guy expression." But then did something she'd never done, not one time since Ben had known her.

She hugged him. Somehow doing it without hurting his bad shoulder. Just put her head on his left shoulder and hugged him.

And said, "You were as big as you've ever been today, Big Ben."

Ben said, "'Bout time."

Lily pushed back now and said, "Winning like that? Did it make all the other stuff worth it?"

"You want to know the truth, Lils? I don't know." Smiled again and said, "But I do know this didn't stink."

"You beat him with *his* favorite shot," Lily said.

"That didn't stink, either," Ben said.

He got into the handshake line with his teammates then, shook hands with the Darby players one by one, Chase in the middle of their line, Ben making sure he treated him the same as everybody else.

Finally.

"Good game," he said.

"You, too," Chase said.

All the "stuff" Lily had just mentioned, including the bad stuff, it still ended in a line like this. After a game like this. Except this time Ben's team had won.

Coach came over to Ben now and said, "You should ice that shoulder as soon as you can. Just sayin'."

"When I get home, Coach. Promise."

"You were great today," Coach Wright said.

"We all were," Ben said. "Isn't that what it's all supposed to be about?"

Coach Wright said, "As a matter of fact, it is."


They had their snacks inside the boys' locker room. As they did, Coach told them again how proud he was of them. Tried to give the game ball to Ben. But as soon as he did, Ben handed it right over to Sam.

Not the first time it had happened.

Then Ben remembered he'd left his long-sleeved shooting shirt behind the bench and went out to get it, not because he was going to want to keep wearing it now that the season was over. Just knowing he wanted to keep it. One more way to remember the year.

Sometimes you didn't need a championship trophy after all.

When he got out to the court, Chase Braggs was there. No way to avoid him. Standing right there in front of the Rams' bench. Obviously waiting there for Ben.

"I just wanted to tell you . . . I'm sorry I knocked you down," he said. "That was over the line."

Put out his hand. Ben didn't hesitate, shook it.

"I didn't have to hit you that hard," Chase said.

"Stuff happens," Ben said.

Thinking: Boy, does it ever.

Ben could see that the kid who had done so much talking all year was having a hard time finding the right words now.

After a long pause Chase said: "I just want you to know something. Where I lived before, before I moved here . . . everybody my age, they always talked about me. I was always the guy, not just in basketball. Baseball, too. Then I moved here and even in Darby, all I heard about was this little guy . . . this *guy* . . . in Rockwell who could, like, do no wrong."

Ben didn't know what to say to that.

"So I decided I had to beat you," he said. "And then I wanted to beat you too bad." Paused and said, "Even with Lily."

Ben grinned and said, "Guess what? I kind of did the exact same thing."

Then: "Hey, good luck in the championship game."

Chase Braggs shook his head, no. "I feel like we just played it today," he said. "And got beat by a point."

Finally he said, "Hey, see you in baseball."

"Cool," Ben McBain said.

Coolest thing in the world, Ben thought to himself, walking over to where Lily Wyatt waited for him.

No matter what, there was always another season.

Just like that, it was baseball season.

## JUST LIKE THAT, IT WAS BASEBALL SEASON. . . .

*Ben, Sam, Coop, Shawn, and Lily return in a third Game Changers novel!*

The Core Four plus Shawn have had an incredible year so far — an unlikely championship win in football and a major moral victory with their basketball team. But baseball is about to begin, and with any new season comes a new set of rivals and challenges. This will be Ben's toughest season yet as he struggles to prove himself as a great friend and leader.

# ACKNOWLEDGMENTS

*For my wife, Taylor, and our children: Chris, Alex, Zach, and Hannah.*

*This one is also for all the kids I ever coached, and the memories they produced, and the stories they made me want to tell.*

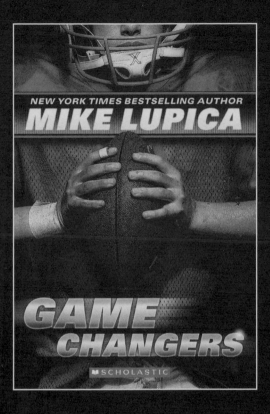

**Read the first Game Changers to see where it all began!**